Moon Rise

KATE DANLEY

Copyright © 2015 Kate Danley

Cover Design by Lou Harper

All rights reserved.

To Laurie Blumberg

who has healed more dogs than a magical berry bush

CHAPTER ONE

Aein clenched and unclenched her fist, trying to ignore the shooting pain radiating up her arm. Over three months had passed since the attack on the Haidra castle. Her broken bones were mended. The bite marks Queen Gisla left when she tore through Aein's skin were now stiff scars. But, much like the rest of the kingdom, Aein wondered if the wounds from that day would ever completely heal.

"Everything all right there, Aein?" asked Lars, lifting his visor and dropping his sword to his side.

The sounds of a melee filled the training yard as the soldiers around them continued to spar. This was the first time she felt strong enough to suit up. To prepare for battle, the guard practiced in full armor, learning how to take a fall and get back up in heavy plate. All Aein could think was how grateful she was for the chill of winter. Otherwise, she was fairly certain she would have rusted her entire suit solid with her sweat. The disciplined Haidra guard was quite different than the ragtag army of the Arnkell stronghold.

Aein swung her arm in a wide, gentle circle, trying to undo the cramp. "Old war wounds," she smiled grimly.

Lars removed his helmet and came over to examine

her. His tall, gangly frame blocked out the sun, making his red hair glow like a halo.

"Did I strike too hard?" he asked with concern.

He took her wrist in his palm as if she were made of eggshell instead of flesh, and turned it this way and that, examining it for any signs that something tore.

She knew she was fine, but let him continue his examination. Lars had been so good to her. He seemed to view her recovery as some sort of personal mission. He was the one who got her up and walking, he was the one who first put a weapon back in her hand. He yelled at the healers when he felt they weren't doing enough, and otherwise teased her and cajoled her and kept her from slipping into despair.

"It's nothing," Aein protested. "Lord Arnkell will not stop to see if I am feeling up to it if he decides to invade again."

Lars let her go. The mention of their former lord's name cast a shadow and Aein wished she could take the words back. The truth rang too loudly to be drowned out by her joke.

Lord Arnkell survived the fight which killed Haidra's king. He retreated to his stronghold and Queen Gisla, deep in grief for her father, let him go.

Aein did not know how Lord Arnkell managed to cobble together enough staff to run his fortress, much less the soldiers needed to protect it from invading forces. In the past, the slightest whiff of weakness caused the surrounding strongholds to transform into jackals, ready to snap the spine of an injured land. Aein was surprised that, after the official funeral of state and coronation, Queen Gisla had not taken advantage of the moment to claim the Arnkell stronghold. But, Aein thought with a sigh, she hadn't. The queen was strong and intelligent, but Aein could not understand her reasoning. Perhaps it was because she had been forced onto an early throne and was still not sure what to do with her power. Perhaps it was because she was a werewolf and didn't know if her people would follow her. Her transformations were whispered and gossiped about, and Aein had to admit that no matter how much she loved her new queen, Gisla's hold on the crown was weak.

This unrest was why Aein rarely saw Finn anymore, the brave commander who saved her life more times than she could count. Every night, when the queen shifted into her wolf form, Finn took her place on the throne. He was the only man powerful enough to keep the kingdom under control until the sun rose again.

During the day, he watched. His shaggy, black body was often hidden in the shadows, catching every scent and word. Nothing escaped him. A high ranking lord was the first to learn Finn was not some mindless beast. A treasonous comment made in front of the werewolf resulted in the man being stripped of his titles and land. It would have cost him his head, but some on the court felt his views on a bewitched ruler were not entirely incorrect.

The other werewolves living at the castle inserted themselves into Queen Gisla's private guard. They lived their lives as humans as best they could, but when the sun set or rose in the sky, they took their place in Queen Gisla's pack.

Finn continued to lead the day wolves, but Queen Gisla replaced Lars as the alpha of the night. There were whispers that this was why Lars became so involved with Aein's recovery - Aein's affection for Lars earned him respect from the pack. All the wolves would lay down their lives for her knowing she freed them from their wildness with her berries. But perhaps, Aein thought as Lars put his helmet back on to pick up where they left off, he helped her because he cared.

But before they could cross swords again, a familiar wolf with a silver scar running across his face trotted towards them.

"I wonder why Finn's here..." mused Aein.

Lars looked over his shoulder and spotted their approaching commander. "Perhaps a social call?"

"You know it is not."

"A man can dream."

The wolf came to a stop and stood before them, fixing Aein with his steady gaze.

"Finn?" she enquired with polite deference, trying hard to preserve the ridiculous formality required of their positions. They had been through too much for the charade to make sense, but order and hierarchy ruled in the guard. The close familiarity they developed saving Queen Gisla had faded into duty. "Can I help you with something?"

The wolf barked and dashed off. Then he came running back again, indicating they should follow.

"Well, that answers that question," sighed Aein. She walked over to the weapons shed and tossed her practice sword down.

"Think of it as the break you were hoping for," said Lars, draping his heavy, soaked arm across her shoulders.

Grimacing, Aein wiggled her way out from beneath him. He laughed and shook his head, his sweat flying everywhere.

"Give me an invading horde! You are disgusting!" she said, wiping herself off.

"Careful, Aein," said Lars. "You may get your wish."

Finn, unamused, barked at them again, urging them to hurry. With a glance, they quickened their pace.

As they followed Finn into the keep, Aein could not help but feel bad for him. He took human form at night when most of the castle was asleep. At least Aein had Lars to lean on. Finn's lifelong friendship with Queen Gisla was gone, reduced to a few short moments when the light intersected at dusk and dawn. It was a miserable existence. Everyone clung to the hope that as soon as the berry bush bore fruit, the nightmare would be over.

They walked up the stone stairs and into the formal

petition room. The throne where Queen Gisla normally sat was empty. Finn led them to a door in the far corner and barked at the guard. The guard pulled the wrought-iron ring and opened it, admitting them into the second petition room. This was a smaller room, but even more grand. The ceiling was painted bright blue with golden stars, a pattern matched in the fabric draping the walls. A recently completed portrait of the fallen king hung opposite of the throne. But Finn did not pause. He continued on to a third door.

Aein gulped. So there was an urgent matter. She glanced at Lars as she attempted to tidy her appearance. He was trying to flatten his red hair. It was a hopeless cause.

This door was guarded by two soldiers. They did not acknowledge Aein and Lars's approach, they just pulled open the heavy carved door.

It was Queen Gisla's private audience chamber. She used it when something actually needed to be done. This throne sat on the floor rather than a dais. It was made for comfort rather than to impress. The discussions in this room often went on for hours.

Queen Gisla waited for them. She wore a gown of white. Her ebony hair was swept up and rolled on either side of her head, her golden crown perched atop. Her neckline was open, and a great red ruby sat against her dark, brown skin.

Aein and Lars fell to one knee and did not lift their eyes until she bid them.

"Arise," she said, motioning with her hand. Finn trotted to Queen Gisla and settled himself at her feet. Aein and Lars stood at attention waiting for the queen to speak.

After a long pause, she said, "There is a matter of great importance which I need you to attend." Her shockingly blue eyes scanned them for any sign of hesitation or betrayal. Though they had sworn themselves to her, they were once members of the enemy's stronghold, a fact no one in the Haidra household forgot. She gripped the arms of her wooden throne. "The entire fate of my kingdom lies upon the blossoming of a bush in Lord Arnkell's territory. As you may or may not be aware, part of our oath when we take our throne is to swear that we will maintain a guard along the border at all times. During the war, Aein and Lars, you were not at your post."

Her words held no accusation, but that did not temper the bite. Aein lowered her eyes and swallowed, feeling like, despite everything, they should have found a way to stay.

"I ordered four members of my guard to the border the day after the battle, to not only protect the bush, but to protect us from any creatures which might try to come through." Queen Gisla sighed and a shadow crossed her face. "Three weeks to the swamp from here, a month at their post, and then three weeks to return. Their replacements were sent and the first deployment should have returned weeks ago. They did not. There has been no word from the other guards. Nothing. And so you see my problem. It may be that Lord Arnkell did not think well of my people patrolling his territory. But it may be that something has come through." Queen Gisla fixed her sight on Lars and Aein. "I need you to go to the Arnkell swamp. You are of the Arnkell land. If it is an issue of territory, you may know the guards your old lord sent. If it is something else, I need to know that, too. Heed my command, though. The border must be held. If all is lost and you must choose, hold the post."

A chill ran up Aein's spine. Other than to gather the harvest to end the werewolves' shift, she never wanted to set foot in the swamp again. A small, strangled sound came from Lars. It was so soft, only Aein heard it. Whatever her fears, Lars had suffered more. He served three tours in the past year, well beyond the safe threshold. He had been trapped there for months, holding the border by himself. He had been driven to the brink of madness. Aein hated to think what might happen if he was sent back.

"The fog will play tricks on our minds," warned Aein. Lars did not add his voice to Aein's words. He just stood there, arms clenched at his side, eyes fixated into space.

"I know," said Queen Gisla, running her hand over Finn's fur, as if needing to soothe herself. Finn gave a bark, as if urging her to keep steadfast in her decision. Queen Gisla turned back to Aein and Lars. "I would not ask, except the need is so great."

It was cold comfort that the queen understood the enormity of her request. She was making it all the same. Aein and Lars fell again to their knees in acceptance of their duty. There was no other choice. They were her soldiers. They were hers to command as she saw fit.

"Stealth shall be your friend," Queen Gisla instructed. "We must not alert Lord Arnkell to your movements. It could be seen as an act of war, and the peace we have is tenuous at best. Prepare yourselves to leave tomorrow at first light. Tell no one of your mission. If there is a possibility that the bush has been lost, we shall have civil war. The only reason I am able to maintain my throne is the promise of my cure in the spring. I will not be allowed to remain queen if they believe otherwise."

Her dire prediction quelled Aein's reservations. Her duty, as guard, was to the people and the Haidra kingdom could not afford more unrest, especially only three months after the damage Lord Arnkell caused. They were still repairing the fortress walls from where the catapult bombarded it. They were still filling in the tunnels he had dug. Not to mention the cost of human life. The price was too high already.

And Aein could not help the unbidden thought from entering her mind... it was a price paid for something she had done. As she and Lars bowed their heads and backed out of the room, she wondered if this mission was her penance. None of this would have happened if she had left the mushrooms in the swamp. She owed it to every surviving man, woman, and child to stop the bleeding, no matter what the personal cost.

As soon as the doors shut in front of them, Aein and Lars stood. No longer in the queen's presence, they turned and walked away, through the empty petition rooms and out into a small courtyard. The walls were windowless. The walkway of the battlement above was empty. With no one watching, Lars closed his eyes, placed his palms upon the plastered stone, and pressed hard.

"We have to go back," he said. His face was haunted.

CHAPTER TWO

A heavy, dappled war horse passed through the dusty bailey to the stables. The plated-steel armor over his head and neck rattled with every step. Aein stepped out of the way. The sky was turning from blue to yellow and Lars was giving his last instructions before the dark stole his human form. The single tower of the Haidra castle rose behind them.

"Talk to Finn," he said. "I am sure he knows everything already, but... make sure he understands what is going on, that he didn't forget... Not that he would. But just in case..."

Aein understood the words he was stammering over. He hoped Finn could stay their execution. Finn knew what the swamp was like. Perhaps if Aein personally made the appeal, Finn would speak for them and find a way to keep them here. Lars reached over and grasped Aein's hand, giving it a desperate squeeze.

"I shall see you in the morning," Aein said quietly as the sun hit the horizon.

The hand in hers faded. Fingertips were replaced by hard flesh, skin replaced with fur, and soon she held not a hand, but a paw. The man beside her disappeared.

The only comfort was that the shift was no longer painful. But as she gazed into the wolf's eyes, she saw her friend inside, trapped in a body he did not want. He withdrew his paw and snorted.

"I shall see you in the morning," Aein repeated again, stroking his shaggy head.

There was a familiarity they shared when he was a wolf that she never would have dared when he was human. It felt natural to rest her hand upon his shoulders, to feel his body lean against her legs. Some nights, they would even curl up by the fire like puppies in a pile. But as humans... she thought back to that battle day when Lars had sworn his love to her. The matter was never spoken of again. Her energy had been devoted to healing and recovery these past months. She wondered what would have happened if she had not been injured, where they would have been. So much of her life was an amalgamation of "what-ifs." What if she had not spotted those mushrooms? What if she had not stopped to eat a berry? What if she had stayed at the border with Lars? Would he have killed her? What if Cook Bolstad, the man who had been a father to her, had never sent her on this devil's errand...

Lars gave another sneeze and headed off to bed. He did not like to be awake during his time as a wolf. He preferred to spend the hours dreaming instead, where he could take any shape he wanted.

Aein turned back towards the castle and was surprised to find Finn resting against a doorway watching her. He wore an indigo tunic over his chainmail. His messy, blonde hair looked like he had rubbed his hands through it a few times after waking. His beard never seemed to grow and was in a state of permanent stubble. The only marked difference between the man he was today and the man she met not so many months ago was the long scar which ran across his face from forehead to cheek, left over from where he brushed against silver ore during transformation.

"How long have you been standing there?" she asked suspiciously.

He stood up, leaning towards her as if he was about to impart some great wisdom. "If you hope to survive, you should instinctually know the answer to that question."

Aein laughed and rolled her eyes. "What can I do for you?" she asked.

He fell in step beside her. "I wondered if I might enjoy your company at dinner. I have a proposal I would like to discuss."

His words caused her to pause. There was something to his tone which made her realize this request was not being made in an entirely official capacity. "Want to give me a hint?"

"Your journey to the border," replied Finn. "Dinner?"

"Absolutely," answered Aein. "Allow me to change."

A bell tolled in the distance, signaling that the gates of the town were being closed for the night. As Aein made her way to the barracks, she thought how the town around Lord Arnkell's fortress was not even organized enough to have a gate. It was just a scattering of houses and shops. She had thought his stronghold was the finest in the world before she came to the Haidra kingdom. She wondered how Lord Arnkell thought attacking this place made sense. All he had to do was marry Queen Gisla and it would have all been his. It was such a waste.

Along the battlements of the castle, the flickering torches colored the darkness. Along with the men who rotated in to take the watch, the shaggy figures of Aein's wolf army changed places. Some of the humans preferred their lives as wolves. Most of them were people whose human bodies ached from age and injury, but in wolf form were strong and whole again. They slept while human and chose to serve whenever the shift came. And then there were those like Lars who were ashamed of their shift, who hid in the shadows and waited for the earth's rotation to take away their four-legged prison.

Aein leaned back her head. The wind was picking up. Storm clouds were rolling across the sky and not a single star lit the black. The moon itself was a mere sliver, barely shedding any light. Tomorrow would be the new moon and everything would be dark. It would make traveling more difficult, but it would also mask them from prying eyes. She hoped no one would notice or care that she and Lars were slipping away.

As Aein entered the building, her metal armor echoed loudly. The barracks consisted of one long room. A row of beds lined the wall in strict precision. At the end of each was a wooden chest for personal belongings. Aein unbuckled her breastplate and let it drop onto her mattress. She stripped off her outer clothes and set them aside for the washerwoman, taking a fresh uniform out of her boot locker. By one of the cots was a jug and basin. She poured out a little water and wiped the day's dirt and sweat from her face.

She nodded in greeting as several soldiers came into the room. Their eyes were ringed with dark circles, and their cheeks were hollow, lacking any mirth. The daily tension was taking its toll. The guard knew this business with Lord Arnkell was not done. They waited and watched the horizon, knowing the wave of war would crest, it was only a matter of when. It was a self-imposed siege.

Aein ran her comb through her snarls and plaited her long, blonde hair into a single braid. She put on her fresh things and strapped a dagger to her side. Ever since the wedding feast, she never went anywhere without a silver knife. She vowed she would not be taken again without warning.

She left the room and made her way down to the banqueting hall. The high beamed ceiling was hazy from the fire pit's smoke. The tables were full of men and women who had just come off duty. Queen Gisla was nowhere to be seen. She had taken to eating in her rooms when in wolf form so her people would not see her ripping and tearing into flesh like an animal. In the early days, someone threw her a scrap from his plate. That man now rotted in the Haidra dungeon.

But other wolves were seated by the fireplace, delicately eating the pre-cut pieces of venison put before them. Lars confessed that in wolf form, the taste of raw meat was as intoxicating as a fine wine. But in the interest of indicating the human intelligence of the werewolves in a kingdom still not comfortable with their bewitchment, Queen Gisla instructed the kitchen to cook the wolves' food as if it was a meal fit for an honored guest. It was served not on the hard slabs of bread used as plates by the rest of the court, but silver and gold platters.

Aein stepped in and all of the wolves stopped to see what she was doing, their eyes fixed upon her for any sign of instruction. She passed by them and they whined to be close to her, pressing their bodies against her legs and putting their large heads beneath her hands.

Finn sat at the head table, to the right of where Gisla sat when she was human. He was tearing into a turkey leg, his face and hands shining with grease. When he spotted Aein, he took a quick mouthful of mead to clear his throat and motioned her over. She sat in the empty seat beside him, uneasy to be at the head table, even if by invitation. She lifted food from the platter in front of her with her fingers and put it on her plate. Finn filled her glass and smiled.

"Good to see you," he said.

"You, too," she replied, digging into her dinner. For a few moments, they ate in silence, enjoying the meal after such a long day.

The immediate pangs of hunger sated, Finn wiped his mouth on the back of his hand and took another drink. "I'm coming with you," he informed her.

Aein put down her roast chicken, choking a little in surprise. "I don't think you can," she reminded him. "Queen Gisla needs you here."

Finn shook his head. "This is not for debate. I am coming with you."

His declaration mystified Aein. "What prompted this?"

"You need two wolves. One who shifts at night, one who shifts at day. Our eyes and ears are better than yours and you need someone to keep watch."

"Yes…" Aein agreed, then pointing out the flaw in his logic, "but the queen of this kingdom needs you here to be her voice when she shifts. I'll take one of the others."

Again Finn cut her off. "You know as well as I that the wolves of night are more wild than those of day. They only received half of the berry. Queen Gisla can keep them in check. But if you were to bring one of them with you, they would challenge you to become alpha of the operation, a fight you don't want to get into in the middle of the swamp with a werewolf."

As if to punctuate his warning, one of the wolves snapped at another who came too close to his meal. True, as a group they deferred to her. But without the pressure of the others to keep the order? To police each other? Aein knew what Finn said was true. "But what about the queen?"

"There are advisors here. There are people loyal to her who have not and will not stop supporting her just because she changes form each night. She has more friends than you. And on this mission, you are going to need all the friends you can get."

It was a simple statement of fact, but it caused a strange warming sensation in her chest. Lars made her strong because she had to be strong for him. But Finn… Finn was his own fortress. He protected everyone around him. She knew he would do anything to keep her safe. Despite her fears of what lay ahead, the thought he would be there made it suddenly bearable.

She had missed him. She had missed her friend.

"Thank you," she said, unable to express her gratitude adequately.

"When do we leave?" he asked, taking another large bite.

"First light," Aein replied. "When the gate to the town opens."

Finn nodded in agreement. "Good. Hopefully I will not be recognized in wolf form and no one will be the wiser."

Out of the corner of her eye, a movement caught Aein's attention. She stood up quickly, her hand upon her knife.

"What is it?" asked Finn.

"I know that man," she replied.

"Who?"

She drew her dagger. A man dressed in a servant's outfit disappeared behind a tapestry. There was a humble room behind it filled with long, wooden tables and benches. It was where the pages of the court waited to be called. The room had a second door down to the kitchen.

Aein strode towards the room, pushed the tapestry aside, and walked through. Finn whistled to the wolves eating by the fire before he followed fast on her heels. The pages stopped their conversations and leapt to their feet.

"Which way did he go?" growled Aein.

The wolves streamed into the room, hackles raised. A terrified boy of fourteen pointed towards the door to the kitchen.

Aein turned to the wolves. "There was a man," she explained, "a man I recognized from the Arnkell stronghold. He went down the stairs. Get him!"

The wolves took off, howling and baying. Aein followed them down the stairs with Finn at her side.

"A spy?" he asked as they ran.

Aein nodded. They reached the courtyard. The storm was building and the torches flickered in the growing wind. The wolves were milling around, trying to catch the spy's scent. Aein scanned the roof. A dark silhouette ran on top of the parapet.

"There!" she cried, pointing.

The wolves were at once running up the stairs towards him, the guards on the wall racing towards him, too.

"I want him alive!" shouted Finn.

The man stopped. He looked left and then looked right. He ducked as an arrow flew by his head.

"He has a hook…" Aein said.

The wall had tall, stone merlons - structures that went up and down the edge like wide teeth. The spy latched his hook in the space between, tied a rope to the bottom, and jumped off the other side.

"He is rappelling down the side of the stronghold!" said Aein in disbelief.

"Fire upon him!" Finn shouted to his archers.

The wolves who had been chasing the spy up the stairs were now coming down. The portcullis was being raised slowly, entirely too slowly. The wolves scrambled beneath the pointed gate as soon as there was room.

"They'll never find him in the city," breathed Aein. Who knew how much the spy heard? Who knew what he would report to Lord Arnkell? She turned to Finn. "We must leave now."

CHAPTER THREE

Aein yanked her bags out of her locker. The guards swore they would scour the city until they found the spy. Her wolves were on the hunt for the man's trail. But there was a feeling in the pit of her stomach that all their searches would fail. She cursed that she had not noticed him sooner, had not called for help faster, had not been able to stop it. A streak of black fur ran into the barracks and stopped by the foot of her bed.

"Lars?" she said, barely acknowledging the wolf as she threw her belongings on the mattress. "New plan. We have to go now."

He cocked his head but then ran over to his space, nudging his own locker open with his nose.

"I won't forget your things," Aein said, wrapping an ax in a blanket and fixing a mace to her side. Since her injury, she had lost the dexterity to wield a sword. Cruder weapons of brute force were the most she could reliably handle. Even so, she stared at her unused arrows, bow, and quiver at the bottom of her trunk. She could not leave them behind. Her hands shook as she picked them up, the adrenaline pounding through her veins. The last time she held them was the day Lord Arnkell stormed the castle.

She had to keep calm, she reminded herself. But all of the ramifications - if the spy revealed where they were off to, if the spy reached the bush before they did, if the people she knew were trapped as werewolves for the rest of their lives - ran through her mind.

She hurried over to Lars's things. He barked at her when she touched something he wanted and growled when she packed something he didn't. Finally, she slipped on her chainmail, strapped her breastplate in place, and grabbed her metal helmet. She bent down to lift both of their bags and almost collapsed beneath the weight. She took a deep gulp of air. She hated that her body didn't respond the way it used to. She hated that she was weak. She called out to a page walking by the door.

"You! Take these things down to the stable and have horses prepared for me," she commanded.

The page took one look at the packs and dashed outside the door to find help. She cursed how they were making this escape. It was supposed to have been done with delicacy and stealth, but now they were madly running around. A hasty departure right after the disappearance of a spy? Who would not leap upon such a juicy bit of gossip to discuss in the city's taverns? But there was no helping it. There was a spy. He was on his way to report to Lord Arnkell. And they needed to leave now.

She strode towards Queen Gisla's private chamber, Lars at her heels. The guards opened the doors as soon as they saw her coming. Again, Aein found herself cursing, knowing that they must have been instructed to give her such ease of entry.

She had never been in the queen's bedroom before. The walls were white plaster, painted with pink and indigo vines. The room was round with alcoves for the canopy bed, prayer room, and fireplace.

But Aein almost ran into Queen Gisla as she entered the room. Finn was at the far end and the she-wolf was blocking him from leaving. He welcomed Aein with a look of frustrated relief.

"Your majesty," said Aein, falling to one knee before rising, even though the wolf did not acknowledge her. "We must be off or your life may be forfeit."

Queen Gisla snapped, her fangs flashing at Aein in anger.

Lars began to growl.

"No, you two," commanded Aein. "We do not have time for this."

But Queen Gisla and Lars began to circle one another, their hackles raised and teeth bared.

"We must go!" Aein pleaded. "Know if there was any other way, we would take it."

Queen Gisla and Lars leapt at one another, fur flying.

"Gods curse it!" Aein swore. She and Finn jumped in to pull the two dogs apart. The air filled with snarling and snapping as Lars and Gisla tried to find a way to get around Finn and Aein.

"Your majesty!" shouted Finn as he tried to grab her by the scruff of the neck.

The queen lunged towards Lars and as she did, her mouth clamped down on Aein's chainmail. Aein instinctively cried out a terrified scream, the memory of when Queen Gisla's jaws broke that bone just a few months ago.

Immediately, the wolves stopped, shrinking back as if they had been struck. Queen Gisla cowered, as if suddenly remembering that her teeth tore at Aein once before. Her animalistic fury was replaced with the horrified memory, or perhaps realization, that she was human and this was the behavior of a wild creature.

"I am unharmed," Aein reassured her, still gripping her forearm. "I am unharmed..."

Queen Gisla hung her head. She tentatively crept to Aein, the embarrassment spoken in every movement. She lifted her snout and touched Aein's fingers apologetically.

Aein rested her hand on Queen Gisla's head and gently stroked her fur, letting her know all was forgiven.

"Finn is your most trusted advisor and you must trust him in this. He swears there are others who are loyal to you and can take his place until he returns. But every moment we have wasted here has put our lives... his life... in danger." Queen Gisla shifted her puppy-like eyes from Aein to Finn and then back to Aein again. "The spy gets further ahead. He heard of our plans. We must get to the bush and protect it before Lord Arnkell gets there. We must find out what happened to the guard. We must..." Aein did not complete the sentence, realizing everything she could say were the words that Queen Gisla used to order her to go in the first place. "You put us in danger to keep us," she finished.

Queen Gisla whined at Finn. He knelt down to run his hands over her face and jaw. "I shall return. You are not abandoned. We go to protect you."

Aein wondered, not for the first time, if their stations had been different, if life had not unfolded as it had, if Finn would have sat beside Queen Gisla on the throne. There was a softness to his spirit, a gentle caring which Aein had only caught a glimpse of a few times in her life. She knew both Finn and Queen Gisla were aware of their place, that they would never do anything to damage the stability of the Haidra kingdom, but Aein wondered.

Queen Gisla seemed appeased, for she rose and leapt onto the bed. She flopped down, placing her head between her paws, and gazed at them with worried eyes. Finn turned to Aein and Lars and gave them a nod. He placed his hand upon his sword and they strode out of the room towards the stables.

They walked in silence, their minds adjusting from the conflict to the duty they now had to embark upon.

"Do you have everything you need?" asked Aein as they swiftly made their way through the hallway, the torchlight flickering.

"We shall find out," replied Finn grimly.

They arrived in the stables and two horses had been saddled and readied. A third horse was loaded with their supplies. Finn reached into his pack and pulled out two cloaks. He handed one to Aein. "Best not to make it too easy to see who travels," he explained.

Aein nodded and put it on, hiding her blonde hair beneath the deep hood. Without a word, they led the horses out and across the bailey to the barbican gate. Lars trotted between them, as if he understood it was best if he remained as hidden as possible. In the dark, he might be mistaken for a small pony. Outside the main castle walls, the city was still busy with revelers. There were many glances. There was no way two soldiers clearly traveling could have snuck out when there was nothing else to provide distraction. The more inebriated gave a tip of the hat and a bob of the head. But there were others, men and women, who glared at them with suspicion and mistrust. A man spotted Lars between them and spat upon the ground.

Aein began to understand why Queen Gisla was so anxious about Finn leaving. She knew tensions were high, that the people of the kingdom did not like the idea of a bewitched ruler. It was as if the darkness gave people the safety to be their true selves, and their true self was ugly.

Finn kneed his horse to the right and led them through the winding roads to one of the secondary gates. It was barred and locked. Finn rode to the gatehouse and pounded on the door. It opened and a sleepy man in a stocking cap rubbed his eyes. "What the blazes to you mean coming here this time of—" His jaws clamped shut as he saw who sat before him. He bowed his head. "My apologies."

Finn held out a parchment. "Open the gate," he said.

The man bowed and scraped his way back inside. Slowly the portcullis rose and they were able to ride beneath.

"The alarm rung in the city for a spy on the loose and that man sleeps abed..." said Finn darkly, glancing over his shoulder as the keeper closed the gate.

He did not complete the thought. If their mission was not so important, their need so dire, the man would have found himself looking for a new job. Was he incompetent or in league with the spy? The gatekeeper would have a few days' grace before Finn dealt with him, Aein thought, trying to believe that they would be back soon.

"Let's keep our pace casual and slow until we get out of sight of the castle," Finn directed. "No need to add to the rumors that we left as if hellhounds were nipping at our heels."

Lars's tongue lolled out the side of his mouth. The grin on his wolfish face said that he was available if they needed such a service.

The countryside around them was quiet and still. The sliver of the moon barely lit their way. Aein thought back to that day when she and Lars first traveled to the swamp. She had been so full of excitement then, so naïve. She wished for those days again. The thought of the fog sent a chill up Aein's back.

"Warm enough?" asked Finn, glancing at her sideways.

She nodded, trying to display the ease and courage he wore as comfortably as a second skin. "Just thinking of what lay ahead."

Finn laughed. "That would be enough to send shivers up anyone's spine."

Aein and Finn fell silent as Lars raced ahead, sniffing the bushes and peering into the darkness. It seemed a false alarm and they both relaxed.

"What is beyond the swamp?" Aein asked him. "We always heard the stories of needing to guard it, but we were never told what lay beyond. What are we protecting ourselves from?"

She was surprised he didn't have an answer for her. "I don't know. No one has ever come back to tell us. But from what's gotten through during just my lifetime, I would hazard it isn't a very nice place."

"Maybe it is a land of indescribable beauty and they keep wondering why all these monsters they are banishing keep coming back," replied Aein.

"Wouldn't that be something?" said Finn, leaning back in his saddle and staring up at the sky.

"How bad do you think it's gotten?" Aein asked, terrified of the answer.

He couldn't meet her eyes. He stared at the stars as if he didn't have enough days left on the planet to gaze upon them. "Bad."

"I only served there for a few days before all of this happened," explained Aein. "I don't know what it's really like."

Memories seemed to flicker across Finn's face, thoughts of things that make a person strong or kills them

"Did you ever see anything?" she asked.

He nodded, wiping his nose as he glanced back to make sure there weren't any followers. "Of course."

"What did you see?"

"Monsters," he said. "Creatures out of your nightmares. They always came at night. Always hid in the fog."

"Were they real?" Aein asked, remembering how the fog played tricks on her, convinced her that there were phantoms when there were not.

"Real enough," said Finn. "Whether they exist in our imaginations or the fog created them, I did not wait to find out. They died like anything else at the end of my blade." He motioned to Lars with a jerk of his chin. "In fact, of all of us, I would say those of us who transform will be at an advantage."

His words gave Aein pause, made the thoughts jumble in her mind as the world shifted just a bit. "Strange that this thing which seems such a curse in our world will actually be useful in the swamp."

"Isn't it?" replied Finn. His horse pranced nervously beneath him, as if all this talk of the swamp was bringing back bad memories for him, too. Finn tightened his seat and patted his mount's neck. "It is only human intelligence which gives us an advantage over the beasts." This time it was Finn who paused. "But with the berries we consumed, we now have both the strength of the beasts and the intelligence of humans."

"Well, then. I hereby elect you and Lars to official defensive duty while I watch the horses," Aein pronounced.

"Oh, you're not getting off that easily," said Finn. "I tell you what..." He bended over to conspire with her. "I have heard you were one of the best chefs in the entire Arnkell stronghold. How about one fully cooked meal for every monster I kill for you?"

The first day Lars and Aein had left for the swamp all those months ago, Lars had made a similar proposition. Aein could not help the smile which crept across her face as she remembered. "Lars promised me two monsters per meal. But give me three and you have yourself a deal."

Finn held up his hands. "Too rich for my blood! I'm afraid you'll have to fight alongside us, instead."

"It appears I have overplayed my hand," she mock groaned. "I suppose I shall have to do what I have been trained for."

The corners of Finn's eyes crinkled as he laughed. Aein hadn't realized how much she missed that sight, how much she missed their easy camaraderie. For a moment, it was as if no time had passed.

Finn looked over his shoulder towards the castle and seemed pleased. "I think we're safe to go a little faster. There is a storm rolling in. Let's get as far along as we can and see if we can find some shelter."

He tapped his heels into his horse's side and they were off. Lars watched them with interest as they passed him by and then raced to catch up. The first gentle drops began to fall. They slowed their horses down, but within an hour, the heavens opened up. The rain beat down incessantly. Aein's cloak kept some of the rain from her face, but as the deluge thickened, it wasn't enough. Rivers of water flowed under her breastplate, the sound of the water striking the metal brim of her helmet made her want to rip it from her head.

Her horse slid badly and she dismounted, fearful he might go down with her on his back. She landed in a puddle of mud up to her ankles. Finn pulled up his mount and came back to Aein.

"Should we make camp?" Aein shouted at Finn over a crack of thunder.

Finn blinked as the rain ran down his scar and into his eyes. "It is too wet to light a fire. At least when we move, we stay warm."

"If we don't find a way to stay warmer, I think moving is going to be a moot point!" she replied.

Finn dismounted and walked by her side. They leaned into the driving wind. The horse slipped again and Aein wondered if they would have to walk all the way to the swamp. It seemed as if they were stumbling along for hours. She could not stop her teeth from clacking together and her body violently shook from the cold. She blew on her fingers to try and warm them. But as she did, she spotted a glimmer of something ahead.

"A light!" she said, lifting up her hand to block out the rain, trying to figure out if it was a lantern or a window.

Finn looked as relieved as Aein felt. "Come on! Let's see if it somewhere we might seek shelter."

"We should proceed with caution!" warned Aein. She had to spit out the water which blew into her mouth.

"The devil himself could be innkeeper and I would gladly sell my soul for a bed," he swore.

Aein looked back at Lars. His tail hung between his legs as the water dripped off his fur. She gave a loud whistle and his head perked up. He trotted over, as if thrilled for any distraction from the misery.

"I need you to go ahead and see what is causing that light," Aein directed.

The wolf gave a sneeze and then took off at a sprint. Aein hoped he would keep his footing. Though the wolves regenerated with each change, they could have a dog with a broken leg until sunrise, and that was not anything they needed in this storm.

Fortunately, Lars returned not five minutes later, dancing around with excitement. He barked and raced back and forwards.

"I think we're in the clear," Aein said to Finn.

"You don't have to be able to speak dog to understand that," he laughed. "Come along! Warm beds await!"

The promise of somewhere sheltered from the rain was just what they needed. Even the horses' steps quickened. The square of light became brighter and brighter.

"An inn!" sighed Aein with relief. Lars let out a bark of agreement.

It was a small, two-story, half-timbered building. The paned glass washed the muddy road with the warm, golden firelight from inside. A dozen travelers sat on long benches, boards heaped with food balanced on their legs. A sign hung to the side of the door with a painting of a cart wheel. There was a muddy path from the inn to a barn filled with bales of hay. They unsaddled their horses quickly and rubbed them down before braving the rain once more. They were a motley crew as they entered.

All eyes turned to the soldiers and the carousing became very still in case this appearance of the Queen's guard was a sign of trouble.

A bald, fat man with a dirty apron stepped forward, a wooden cup in his hand. His mustache twitched as he spoke. "May I help you?"

"We seek shelter," said Finn.

It was then that Lars entered the room. The other guests recoiled, raising their weapons and preparing for attack. The air filled with the smell of wet dog and fear.

Aein motioned with her hand for Lars to sit, and he did. But instead of relieving the tension in the room, a wave of hostility and suspicion spread across it.

"He's with you?" the innkeeper asked Finn.

"He is."

"He's not welcome here."

A single growl rose from Lars's throat. Aein glared at him to get in line. He was not helping the situation.

"In the name of Queen Gisla," said Finn, "he is, indeed, welcome." He pulled out that same parchment which caused the gatekeeper to open the town gate. The innkeeper took one look at the red seal and shut his mouth. But Finn took a sack of money from his belt and placed it in the man's hand. "She hopes this will ease any inconvenience."

The innkeeper wet his lower lip with his tongue, the lure of the money overcoming his discomfort. "You all may stay down here in the central room. I'll not have fleas in my beds."

"Too late!" shouted a man from the back.

At once, the tension dispelled and conversation returned to normal, but eyes still shifted towards them suspiciously. Aein noticed two men slip out the back door. There was something about them which caused the hairs on the back of her neck to prickle.

"I'll see to the horses," Aein whispered to Finn. He gave an imperceptible nod before allowing a wide grin to spread across his face as he announced, "Drinks are on the queen tonight! Open a cask for our new friends, innkeeper!"

The mood in the room shifted again to something more jovial. Aein didn't stay to watch it. She opened the door and stepped out, noting that Lars was with her. She crept towards the stable, grateful Lars was there to serve as her lookout. There were shadows and hidden corners her human eyes could not see in the night. He was alert, but not tense, and she took that as a good sign.

Inside the barn, the two men were saddling their mounts. They left the door open, most likely to make a quick getaway. Aein tiptoed in and hid behind a stack of hay.

"How did they find us?" one of the men said. Aein wondered who found them and what caused them to worry about being found out.

"It is those helldogs," said the other. "Lord Arnkell said they can track a man twenty leagues through a river. They probably smelled us from the road and led those soldiers here."

Aein swallowed, her mouth suddenly dry at the mention of Lord Arnkell's name. She strained to hear more. They were talking low and the sound of their saddles and stirrups clanked over their words.

"If you hadn't gotten yourself seen there at the castle—"

"That wasn't my fault. I don't know how that girl recognized me."

"You should have been more careful—"

"He'll want to know they're here. We have to get there before they do."

Aein pressed herself into the corner of the stall as the men walked their horses out. One gave a nervous whinny, most likely smelling Lars.

"Stinks like a dog in here," said one of the men as he left. Aein thought to herself he had no idea how close he had come.

What to do? she wondered. Should she let Lars loose on them right now? Go after them and question them? Or hurry to the swamp to fortify their defenses around the berry bush?

She rushed out of the barn. The men were disappearing down the road, swallowed by the torrential rain and darkness. She turned to Lars. "Wait here. I'll be back."

She raced towards the inn and tried not to fling the door open. Finn saw her come in and must have seen on her face that things were not right. With a hearty laugh and a backslap, he got up from his seat, carrying his drink with him and sloshing most of it on the floor. Aein knew his tricks.

She stayed next to the door, her back against the plaster wall. He smiled, placing his hand beside her head, and leaned into her.

"What are you doing?" she hissed.

He ran a strand of her hair through his fingers, drinking her in with is his blue eyes. "To anyone looking at us, it appears I'm just a man talking to a beautiful woman the way that men and women talk when they have had too much to drink, as opposed to a commander receiving vital information from a member of his team."

The closeness of his body made her heart skip a beat. She pressed her cheek against his to whisper in his ear, the stubble of his beard rough against her soft cheek. "Two men. Loyalists to Lord Arnkell, one of them was the spy. They have gone to warn him of our location."

Finn ran his hand down her arm and she could not help the shiver which ran up her spine. He interlaced his fingers in hers. "Is Lars outside?"

She pulled her head back, her lips a breath away from his, and nodded.

Finn opened the door, still holding Aein's hand like lovers sneaking off. Aein allowed him to lead her out into the stable. As soon as they entered, Aein stepped away.

"Those two men on the road," Aein commanded Lars. "Track them. Take them down. Do not allow them to reach their destination. "

The fur on Lars's back rose as a wildness came into his eyes. Despite the sanity the berry brought, he was still a wolf after the sun went down and Aein had given him the freedom to do what he did best — hunt.

Without pause, he was gone, sliding into the darkness

like a shadow.

A half-hour passed, but Lars had still not returned. Finn kept pacing to the door and back again. Aein sat upon a pile of hay, clasping and unclasping her hands.

"Do you think he is all right?" she asked.

Finn ran his hand over the back of his neck and looked out into the night. "Of course," he said. "He cannot be killed except by silver or dismemberment."

"Except they know about werewolves," said Aein. "I overheard them."

"He'll be fine," repeated Finn, almost more to himself than Aein.

"We should have gone with him..." she said.

"We would die in that storm."

"Details."

He gave a small chuckle and rubbed his eyes. "What a day!" He threw up his hands. "We are utterly useless to him. Let's get some sleep so at least someone is rested tomorrow."

He reached out to Aein to help her to her feet. She chewed her lip as they walked back towards the inn, nervously glancing down the road, hoping Lars would suddenly appear. The rain had slowed to a trickle. Finn opened the door. Most of the other guests were already settled into their makeshift beds. The innkeeper jumped up from his stool and shut the door behind them, pulling in the latch. "Just waiting until you got back to close up. Wasn't sure if you'd be coming back in tonight."

"Just getting the horses bedded," replied Finn, giving the man a sly wink.

The innkeeper did not particularly care. He motioned to the floor. "Make yourself as comfortable as you can." And then he was gone.

There were other travelers in the room settling in. Most everyone had stripped down to their shifts to get their outer garments dry. Tunics and leggings hung before the fire and on the backs of chairs. Aein followed suit, stripping off her armor and chainmail and setting it to the side. From her bag, she pulled out a jar of bear grease and rubbed it on the links, hoping it would keep the metal from rusting if it had not already begun.

Finn rolled his bed out next to the far wall. He blocked it from prying eyes by placing a bench between him and the rest of the room, then draped it with his wet clothes. The care he was taking gave Aein pause. She realized he was worried about someone seeing him change into a werewolf when the sun rose. Aein walked over and placed her bed beside his and climbed inside the blankets. He raised an eyebrow.

"Just keeping the charade going," she whispered with a wink.

A slow smile crept across Finn's weathered face as he realized she was setting up a secondary line of defense, ready to shield him if necessary. He tucked his feet inside his blankets and pulled the scratchy wool up to his chin.

Aein rested her head in the crook of her arm. "Do you think he caught them?" she asked.

"I cannot imagine him not," said Finn softly.

"I hope he is safe."

The flickering firelight played across the shape of Finn's lips. She thought back to that night so many months ago when they had shared a moment alone, when things had been soft and tender between them. They had not had a moment together like that since, duty always coming between them, any moment interrupted by some task.

"I am glad you're here," whispered Aein.

"Me, too," he replied. His eyes became distant. "You two would have probably been fine on your own, but I had to make sure Queen Gisla…"

His voice trailed off and he did not complete the sentence. Aein tried not to sigh. He would always place the queen first. Though the queen would have to marry for political reasons and there was no hope for any sort of future, especially with one being a wolf at night and one at day, Finn cared deeply for her.

Still, Aein could not help but think back to that one night and wish she could close the distance between them.

Interrupting her own thoughts, Aein focused on the duty before them to distract herself. "What do you think Lord Arnkell has been doing all this time?"

"Raising followers?" Finn gave a small, powerless shrug. "Preparing to finish the war he started? This will not end until one of them is dead."

Aein knew as long as there was breath in his body, Lord Arnkell would fight. She thought back to all the carnage in the stronghold the night he poisoned his people, the way he was willing to slaughter everyone in order to bring down Queen Gisla. Aein's thoughts flickered to finding Cook Bolstad dying in his kitchen, the injuries he had sustained, the way this man she had sworn to protect had forced the only father she could remember to pick between her life and the life of the castle. And Cook Bolstad had chosen that he would rather an entire stronghold die than sacrifice Aein.

"Let's make sure it is him," said Aein.

CHAPTER FOUR

Aein awoke to awareness that Finn was shifting. Her eyes were open in a flash and fixed upon him, ready to hear any last minute instructions before he changed. But it was too late. He opened his mouth to speak just as his mouth became a muzzle. Aein sighed and reached out, stroking his fur gently. He gave her cheek a friendly lick. The morning always came too soon.

She sat up and pushed back her bedding. Every muscle in her body ached from riding. The other people in the room were still fast asleep. She instinctually felt like it was important no one noticed that Finn was missing. Two bedrolls, one of them occupied by a wolf, would seem suspicious. She rolled up the sheets and blankets and tied them together. She checked on her garments. They were dry. She packed their belongings and opened the door, hoping to find Lars waiting outside.

Water dripped from the leaves and the ground was still muddy, but the rain had stopped. At least their misery would be manageable as they traveled. But a kernel of anxiety took root in her gut. There was no sign of Lars. She told herself he was probably waiting for them up the road and not to panic yet.

"Stay!" said the innkeeper coming down the stairs. "I was on my way to cook breakfast." He scanned the room. "Where is your friend with the scar?" he asked.

Aein cursed that Finn had made himself so noticeable the night before. "He went on ahead," she replied.

"Really?" asked the innkeeper with some suspicion. "I did not hear him ride out."

She flashed him an embarrassed smile. "Headed out in the middle of the night. Bit of a lovers' spat." Finn licked her fingers and she batted his mouth away.

The man seemed to accept her excuse in part. "Now what could you do to anger a man like that?"

Finn looked up at Aein and cocked his head, waiting for Aein's answer. Aein would have sworn he was enjoying himself. "People change," replied Aein. "Now, about that breakfast?"

The man hustled to the fireplace. Hanging over the coals from a metal hook was a black cauldron. He lifted the lid, spooned a mound of porridge onto a plate, and handed it to Aein. It was better than what she had in her saddle bag and filling enough. She ate half and put the rest down on the ground for Finn to finish. She was glad to be done and on her way. She hoped no one cared there were three horses to one rider now.

The road was a mess, but not like last night. The storm seemed to have moved on, but the sky was a milky shade of white. The dead grass on either side was the color of straw. The forest beyond was filled with pine trees and scrub. A woodpecker hammered away in the distance.

She kept the horses moving at a slow pace and she was glad she did. Finn gave a whine and stopped. Running towards them through the woods was Lars, his red hair flashing against the forest like a beacon. A wave of relief washed over Aein.

He leaped onto the wet road and slid, stopping himself by grabbing Finn's horse. "This mud!" He swung himself up. "I thought my legs would fall off," he groaned, leaning across the horse's neck.

"Care to report, soldier?" she asked.

"After I get a nap," he replied. "Tie me to my saddle so I don't tip out, would you?" he asked.

She gave him a shove. "Report first! Sleep later."

Lars became serious. "I only got one. The other escaped."

From the look on his face, it was not for a lack of trying. Finn came over and rested his head on Lars's boot. Lars bent down to greet him.

"They were both on horseback," he said. "By the time I did what had to be done, the other was long gone. I tried to catch his scent, but the rain washed it away."

"Is the first dead?" she asked.

Lars nodded, scratching Finn behind the ears. "It will look like an animal attack."

Aein shivered, remembering Lord Arnkell's keep after the wedding feast. "Thank you."

Lars didn't say anything for a moment, just clicked his heels and the horses plodded forward. Finally, he said, "I hate doing that, especially now that I can remember it all."

Aein never thought about it before. The berries brought sanity to the werewolves, but they also brought the ability to remember what happened when they were in wolf form. Prior to ingestion, no one could remember what it was like before and after the shift. It was what made the wolves so dangerous. One moment they were running away from one another, the next, they became the very creatures they were running away from.

"I am sorry we asked that of you," said Aein apologetically. "Are you all right?"

Lars's face hardened and Aein realized she should not have asked him a question which sounded like she doubted his ability to do his duty. "Of course," was all he replied, shutting down.

But Lars always had it more difficult than the other wolves. He had eaten the berry while in human form, so he had been aware of the shift into wolf and how he did not want to become such a beast. He had not had the berry as a wolf and then remembered the relief of becoming sane.

Lars's eyes became distant as the sound of the morning larks sang around them. "Sometimes I wonder what life would be like if none of this ever happened."

Aein knew he did not mean it towards her, but it hit her hard. The fact of the matter was that she was the reason all of this came to pass. She was the one who found the mushrooms Cook Bolstad requested. If she had not paused to collect them, perhaps they would all be sitting in the stronghold. Perhaps her best friend would not be turning into a wolf whenever the dark of twilight fell.

"I am sorry," she replied again.

Lars waved her off, as if realizing where her mind was headed and stopped her from going there. "I only say it because I know others must feel the same. It is a strong rallying point for Lord Arnkell. All he has to do is promise that he will wipe the 'Cursed Werewolves of the Haidra Kingdom' from the face of the earth, and he has an army of followers, including those two spies who were willing to die for him. All he has to do is promise a return to normal and people will do anything."

"He tried to kill us!" pointed out Aein. "He poisoned his own people. He decided to destroy his entire land rather than join with the Haidra kingdom. If you were not a soldier," asked Aein, "would you follow a man like him?"

"A chance to go home? A chance for everything to be the way it was? Even if it meant serving a monster?" Lars mused out loud. He shrugged. "I probably would."

CHAPTER FIVE

They rode in silence for the rest of the day. The storm seemed to have done its worst. There were a few showers, but nothing like before. They were fortunate they did not get the snow and sleet of the more northern lands, but Aein was grateful for the cloak Finn had passed along to her the night they left.

They encountered almost no one on the road. Those they did scowled at them with suspicion. The fighting between the Haidra Kingdom and Lord Arnkell's land had taken its toll. Aein hated that the people they passed were drawn and hungry, their eyes were hardened, their spirit stooped beneath the ravages of this pointless war. All this suffering was because of one man's greed. One man who was willing to sacrifice whatever and whomever he needed to get what he wanted. She hated him.

It was on the fifth day that Finn stopped and raised his nose to the sky.

"What is it?" Aein asked, as if he could answer while in wolf form. Lars pulled out his sword, sensing the shift in mood. His horse danced nervously.

Finn whined. He pointed his nose and paw like a hunting dog. She peered into the shadows of the trees.

"There is nothing there but some birds," she said in confusion.

Finn barked. Aein didn't know if that meant there was someone else there or something else entirely.

"Let's go take a look," said Lars.

Aein's heart skipped a beat as her body prepared for whatever lay waiting in the forest edge. By the time she removed her mace, Finn had taken off into the tree line and Lars was fast behind. She couldn't believe they had gone on without her. She spurred her horse on.

Both Lars and Finn were stopped beneath a tree staring up at one of the higher branches. There was nothing there but a hawk. It would land and then fly off and then come back again. Whenever it moved, Finn began barking and snapping at it, trying to climb up the trunk.

"The hawk?" she said with confusion.

Finn would not leave it alone, so she replaced her mace and pulled her bow from the quiver attached to her saddle. But before she could load the arrow onto the string, the bird was gone, well out of range.

She replaced her weapons and Finn sat, exhaling a disgusted huff. She could see he was frustrated. She turned to Lars. "Any idea what that was about?"

Lars shrugged, as mystified as she was. He pointed at Finn. "We talk tonight," he stated, as both a promise and a threat.

As they returned to the road, Finn kept whining and trying to lead them back into the forest.

"Finn, unless we are in dire danger, traveling through the forest will only slow us down and honestly, not going to provide us shelter. If you haven't noticed, we're wearing this." She banged on her metal breastplate. "Lord Arnkell doesn't need to send any spies. He can probably hear us coming with all this clanking armor."

Finn was not dissuaded and kept running back and forth to the tree line.

"What on earth has gotten into him?" asked Lars,

leaning forward on his saddle. "It is as if he has gone mad."

Aein followed Finn's gaze to the top of one of the trees and squinted. "Is that the same hawk?"

Finn went wild barking and snapping. Aein again pulled out her bow and arrow, but again, before she could even notch it, the hawk took off. But he did not fly away completely. He circled and then came back, landing in a tree some distance ahead. There, he sat and watched them.

"Is that creature following us?" Aein wondered out loud. As soon as she said the words, Finn calmed. "That is what was going on, wasn't it?" asked Aein.

Finn barked in affirmation.

Lars wiped his face with his hand and stared off at the bird. "What can we do about this?" he mused.

Aein put her bow and arrow within easy reach. "We keep an eye on the sky and if it comes close, we kill it."

"But why is it tracking us?" said Lars. "Who sent it? And what knowledge could they glean from a bird? It can't talk. It can't tell anyone what it sees."

"Unless they are able to see what it sees. Or…" Aein looked from Lars to Finn and back again. "Or if the bird is a human, someone capable of shifting into an animal other than a wolf."

Lars clenched his jaw, the muscles bunching at the corners. "Then perhaps it is best if we wait until sunset and see if our friend is still with us when the dark comes."

CHAPTER SIX

The horses grazed as Aein, Finn, and Lars sat beneath the trees, watching the bird and waiting. An hour before the sun hit the horizon, the hawk flew off.

Lars was picking apart a piece of grass and threw it on the ground. "It must need to get back to its master before the change."

"How far can a hawk fly in an hour?" Aein wondered out loud.

"Far."

"Spies everywhere," said Aein, shivering. She rose to her feet. "We should travel as far as we can while the hawk is gone," she replied.

They climbed onto their horses and clicked their heels, spurring them into a gallop to take advantage of the last of the light.

As the horses pounded beneath them, Lars shouted, "We aren't going to make the border anytime soon if we can only move the hour before and after the sun!"

"Stop cheering me up!" said Aein.

Lars laughed and let out a whoop. "We'll never arrive at this rate!"

They rode as hard and as fast as they could until the

sun was moments from touching the treetops. They slowed their horses to a walk and dismounted.

Finn began to shift. His furry body disappeared and he reappeared as a clothed man, crouched upon the ground. He stood and stretched.

"Thanks for the alert on the hawk," said Lars, handing him the horse's reins.

"Someone has to pull his weight around here," joked Finn before becoming serious. "You can smell the shifter. It is like a person, but overhead. Probably why the horses are never afraid of us werewolves. We smell just like people."

Lars folded his arms and ran his thumb thoughtfully across his lower lip. "I'll keep a watch."

"If the hawk comes back," said Aein, "Do we go on or wait?"

Finn rubbed his hands over his shorn, blonde hair. "We'll need to sleep at some point," he said. "My vote is to go until it shows up, then make camp. Preferably next to a crossroad. We won't be able to lose it unless there is cover overhead from the trees, but maybe we'll get lucky."

Aein nodded. There was nothing more to say, for at that moment, the sun dipped below the horizon and Lars began to change. His face became heartbreakingly sad as he watched his hands fade into paws and his limbs replaced. When the transformation was complete, he let out a heaving sigh.

"I know, Lars," said Aein, coming over to him to wrap her arms around his neck. She held his muzzle in her hands. "I promise we shall get a harvest so bountiful that you shall never have to transform again. I promise." He gave her a gentle lick on the cheek and she laughed. She stood, walked to her horse, and mounted. Finn joined her on the horse which Lars had been riding.

They clicked their heels and the horses were off, taking advantage of the last of the light before the twilight swallowed the road and made travel impossible. Aein tried to spot any sign of something flying above. About an hour later, Lars gave a low growl and a bark. Both Aein and Finn stopped their horses.

"Do we have a new friend?" asked Aein.

Lars barked again. It seemed so silly to ask him a question when he could not answer her back.

"Lars," said Finn, leaning forward in his saddle. "Bark twice if it is another shifter."

Lars barked twice.

"You're brilliant," Aein said to Finn.

Finn shrugged. "I kept hoping you would figure out there were ways of asking me 'yes' and 'no' questions."

"I can't believe we didn't think of it before."

Finn dismounted. "Well, we have a new companion. Owl, perhaps?" he wondered. "We'll move out at first light when it flies away. Besides," he yawned, "I'm exhausted. Aren't you?"

Aein could not argue. Their stay at the inn seemed like years ago instead of just a week. They still had another two weeks before they would arrive at the edge of the swamp. Finn began pulling the bedrolls off the horses as Aein gathered firewood. They found a flat area with a spot for the horses to graze. Lars dug the fire pit with his paws while Aein and Finn stomped the grass around it flat. It would make a nice cushion when they slept.

"We should hunt for game if we have the chance," observed Finn. "I don't know what chance we'll have in the swamp."

Unsaid was that they probably would not want to eat anything they caught in the swamp anyways. After the mushrooms, Aein was terrified what other magic they might stumble across.

"I wonder how owl tastes..." Aein commented. Their feathered spy did not reveal himself.

"Stringy," said Finn.

Lars got up for first watch. As Aein and Finn climbed into their bedrolls, Lars reluctantly left to do his patrol, dragging his feet as he went. It had been another long day, but Lars's gloom seemed more pronounced. Aein wondered if she should go after him.

"We should be able to tell if we are getting closer or further from whomever is spying on us based upon the length of time it takes for the birds to come back," observed Finn.

"I am hoping we are getting farther away," said Aein ruefully.

"You and me both." Finn glanced at where Lars disappeared. "Is he okay?" he asked.

Finn was relaxed, leaning on his bedroll on one elbow, tearing off a piece from the dried jerky in his hand. He was so casual, Aein knew that his question was anything but.

"I don't know," she replied. The light of the fire pitched everything beyond it into a dark haze, and Aein didn't know if Lars was sitting within earshot or far away. "It has been difficult for him. I know he will be grateful when this is done."

Finn nodded. "He's had it rougher than any of us. I hate that he's going back into the swamp again so soon."

It dawned on Aein that in addition to Finn's argument that she needed wolves around the clock to protect her in the swamp, perhaps he was also so insistent because he was scared of what Lars might do once he faced the fog again.

"He'll be fine," Aein replied, not convinced of her own words, but feeling like she needed to stand up for her friend.

Finn gave her a soft smile. "It is not weakness to fear the swamp," said Finn. "I want to make sure he knows we are here to help him, that he doesn't have to put on a strong face if he's falling apart. I'd rather know the truth and help him than have it destroy him."

Aein rolled onto her stomach and rested her head on her hand. The grass crunched beneath her. "I was only there for a few days," she said, "and I don't want to go back. I can't even imagine what happened to him out there alone for those months."

"The shift is probably the only thing that kept him alive."

Aein shrugged. "He killed people he knew. I think there is a part of him that wishes he was the one who died."

"I hope he's not carrying around guilt for something he is not responsible for... for something he doesn't even remember."

"But he knows he did it. And for Lars? That's enough."

The fire crackled. "Then we must make sure he knows he is more than that. His life adds up to more than one chapter, no matter how terrible it might have been. It is the rest of his days which define him."

"I hope he figures that out," said Aein.

"And how about you?" asked Finn, with the same casual nonchalance. "How are you holding up?"

Aein stretched her fingers in her hand. She was still so weak, so unable to fight like she used to. "It aches," she said.

"But how about your head?" asked Finn.

Aein tried to smile, but failed. "It aches, too."

"You are more than one moment, too, you know," he replied. His voice was as warm as the fire they laid beside.

"I keep telling myself that," said Aein. "But I keep thinking if I had just made a different choice, none of this would have happened. I could have prevented it all."

Finn nodded. "You're right."

His agreement took Aein aback. "You're not going to tell me that I am being ridiculous?" she challenged.

"Isn't that what you want to hear from someone? That it is all your fault? That if you just learn what you did wrong well enough, this won't ever happen again? And what was the lesson? Not to trust people? Not to trust those you love?"

Aein shifted uncomfortably. "That's not what I am saying…"

"If you are responsible, it means that you have some control over this situation. And isn't that what you want? The ability to stop it?" asked Finn, gazing at her without judgment.

His words struck too close to the truth. Aein's throat tightened and she couldn't look at him.

"It was my greatest wish when I was in your shoes," he said kindly.

"You've been through something like this?" she asked, unbelieving that someone as strong and put together as Finn could have ever made a mistake as huge as hers.

His brow furrowed. A log crackled, spewing sparks into the air. "I'm not much older than you, Aein, and here I am, the commander of the Queen's forces. Of course. Of course I have made a decision which went disastrously wrong." Finn ran his hand over his stubble. His eyes became distant with the memory. "Your stronghold and mine, this whole wedding business between Queen Gisla and Lord Arnkell, it was because of outside threats. The Haidra Kingdom has been at war since I was a child. I was practically given a sword before I was weaned. My first few battles went well. I moved up through the ranks as the anointed golden boy. But then… one time I was supposed to lead my troops on an attack. I saw an opening, or what I thought was an opening. Every man under me perished. The sound of their cries still wake me at night. I survived, though. Managed to be in the right place at the right time to kill their king, which won us the war. I was decorated a hero." Finn laughed grimly. "Can you imagine? Watching your friends get cut down because of a decision you made, and then being rewarded for it? Every day I woke up and I wanted to die."

"What did you do?" asked Aein.

"Queen Gisla's father sat me down and had this talk

with me, the same as I'm having with you. You think it is rough for people like us? Imagine if every decision you make causes a chain reaction like that every day. I had the one battle. Gisla's father was responsible for all of them. Sometimes the only comfort is knowing you aren't alone — that there are others who have been through it and they kept getting up and breathing even if they didn't feel like it. Sometimes they even experience a little bit of happiness again. Gisla's father promised me that if they could do it, I could do it. And it means you can do it, too." His eyes locked with Aein's and a gentle smile crept across his mouth. There was no mirth to it. Just quiet understanding. "You can't prevent a future you can't see. All you can do is promise yourself that you will do everything in your power, even if it destroys you, to heal the wounds you caused. There will be people you love who will make terrible mistakes, and you need to be able to show them how to survive. If you learn any lesson, Aein, learn that. Learn how to survive so you can pass it on."

Aein wiped the tears from her cheeks. "If her father meant so much to you, how could you leave Queen Gisla behind?" Aein asked. "Don't you love her?" The question came out of her mouth before she could stop it. Yes, Finn had given her his official reasons, but there was a part of her that wanted him to have a different answer.

He wet his lips. "She loves me, Aein," he confessed. "But she has to marry. There must be an heir to the throne. Until there is a child in place to take over when she dies, until that line of succession is secure, the kingdom will fall. I had to leave so that she could learn to love someone else."

"And you?" she asked. Aein wanted him to say he came because he needed to be with her. She wanted him to say that he wanted more. How could he know her so well and be so far away? "Have you learned how to do that? To love someone else?"

Finn smiled again, but this time it was full of mystery. The whole world seemed to fade outside of his merry blue eyes and there was only the two of them. Aein's pulse raced as he seemed to gather his thoughts. His lips parted, as if about to utter everything she wanted to hear. She ached for him to reach out and gather her up in his arms, to say that he still thought of that night they had on the road together and he was here because he wanted to see if it could last a lifetime.

And then Lars stepped back into the camp.

He snuffled around the ground and with a huff, curled up beside Aein.

And the moment was lost.

Finn put his head down and suggested, "We should get some sleep."

CHAPTER SEVEN

The hawk continued to follow them and the owl took over at night. Aein, Finn, and Lars had long since abandoned trying to outwit the birds. No matter what side route they took, no matter how they tried to hide their steps, the birds always found them.

The length of time between when the raptors disappeared and when they arrived at first shortened as Aein, Finn, and Lars crossed into Lord Arnkell's land, and then lengthened as they made their way to the swamp.

"So do you think that means Lord Arnkell is tracking us?" mused Lars as the hawk appeared once more in the sky. Finn gave a deep throated growl.

"It follows logic," replied Aein, but she almost choked on the words. There was an insistent voice inside of her that said it was not the case at all.

Places for birds that large to land became sparse. The pine gave way to the bare branches of scrawny trees. The birds spent their time circling high overhead. Aein tried to shake the feeling they were being watched like a buzzard watches carrion.

Lars ran his long fingers through his wavy, auburn hair. Even though it was winter, his pale skin had freckled from all the time outdoors. "You would think Lord Arnkell would be grateful that we're trying to pick up the pieces he dropped."

"Perhaps that is why he has not yet attacked. Perhaps as long as we are headed towards the swamp, he will leave us alone."

"That would require him to actually feel gratitude," Lars pointed out. "And I have to say that in all my years living at the stronghold, that was never a quality I saw in him."

Aein couldn't argue.

"I wonder what he wants," mused Lars.

Aein thought back to the night that Lord Arnkell left her to be ripped apart by the wild wolves. If it had not been for Lars and Finn, she would have been dead. While he tied her to the tree, one of his men had eaten a berry from her bag. She wondered if Lord Arnkell had put the pieces together and figured out why one of his werewolves had gone sane.

Lars shifted in his saddle. "How much further do you think we have to go?"

"You tell me. You've been here more often. I was usually traveling this road on galloping horseback."

"We could gallop a bit," mentioned Lars.

The time on the road seemed both a luxury and a prison. She could not wait to get off of her horse day after day. But she knew what waited for them at the end, and that made every moment spent outside of the swamp a thing to be relished and enjoyed.

Finn was busy scouting ahead. From time to time, he would check in on them, his silvery scar stark against his black fur. But from his relaxed gait, it felt like there was nothing to worry about.

"Let's go," said Aein.

They clicked their heels and were off at a fast pace. The wind was in their face. The gloom of the prior days dissipated. There was nothing but the joy of the ride.

But that was when the trees disappeared. They pulled their horses to a walk and Aein chewed the inside of her lip. She knew they were close, she just did not realize how close. The land had given way to the marsh outside the swamp. The dirt road changed to the wooden piers built through the bog. Even fearless Finn stopped, as if the wolf had to summon his courage to keep going.

Aein squinted. The falcon was there watching them. As she urged her horse forward, the falcon took off in the opposite direction.

"It appears it saw what it needed to see," noted Aein.

"Not even a spy is getting paid enough to go into a swamp," commented Lars.

"I suppose they figure whatever we find in there, we deserve," replied Aein, trying to ignore the pounding in her chest. She looked over at Lars. He was so pale. "Are you ready?" she asked.

He nodded. "It is not going to get any easier." He reached behind and got his helmet from his bag, fixing it upon his head. "Would hate to have something drop out of the swamp and knock me out of my saddle…"

They proceeded in silence, the emptiness of their horses' hooves muffled on the wood of the road. As they approached the mangroves of the swamp, it was like the fog had been waiting for them the entire time. The old pains in Aein's body began to ache, like a rainstorm was rolling in. It was as if the fog knew where her weakness was and how to make her hurt.

Lars pulled his horse to a stop and slumped forward. Aein reached out to him, resting her hand upon his back.

"Are you all right?" she asked, gently.

He nodded, swallowing as if trying to fight down nausea. "It just struck me harder than I expected," he replied. There was a vulnerability to him, this big, strong man struggling to find the courage to go back into this place of nightmares.

Aein stroked his arm. "Take all the time you need."

The relief washed across his face when he understood she accepted this moment not as a sign of weakness, but as an appropriate reaction to their situation. He breathed deep.

Finn sat at the entrance to the swamp, waiting for them. Lars looked up and spotted the wolf. He shouted, "Show off!"

Finn gave a bark, and then bent down as if getting ready to play.

"Can't let myself be shown up by some dog," muttered Lars, pulling himself together. "Let's go in."

He clicked his heels against the side of his horse, who had picked up on the mood. It shied and tried to dance away, but Lars gripped with his legs tightly and steered it back. The horse reared up, trying to unseat him, but Lars pressed on.

"Go ahead!" said Lars to Aein. "Maybe it'll follow if it sees everyone else is going in."

Aein rode her horse towards the entrance, leading the pack horse behind. It didn't seem to help. Lars's horse was still bucking, but then suddenly, it bolted.

Blinded by panic, the horse must have thought the bog around them was firm soil. It ran off the road and the mud swallowed the animal up to its belly. Lars leaped off to try and remove some of the weight, sinking in to his thighs. He grabbed the horse's reins and tugged its head back towards the road. Even though death was at their door, the horse bucked and struggled, preferring to disappear beneath the surface of the bog rather than face whatever was in the swamp.

Aein's heart was in her throat watching Lars fight this struggling animal. She spurred her horse towards them, hoping she would get there in time. She leaped off of the back of her steed and ripped through her saddlebags looking for the rope to throw to them. Her hands shook as she opened the ties. She told herself that Lars did not survive everything he had endured just to die because of some terrified horse. She told herself that she would get him out. But the animal would not be calmed.

Time morphed - to stretch into forever while seeming like it sped up. She was sure years had passed and there was no way they could still be alive. It had only been moments, though. She grabbed the rope, tied it around her saddle, and threw the end to Lars. He grabbed it and looped it around his horse's head. If they could just get the animal going in the right direction, it would be all right, she kept telling herself.

It was then Finn took matters into his own hands. He ran out on the boardwalk and then, with a mighty leap, he jumped into the bog. Aein stifled back a cry as she saw the wolf's body sink, but he struggled on, coming up behind the horse to herd the animal towards safety. Horses and werewolves usually were neutral with one another. The wild werewolves only hunted human flesh and the horses seemed to have figured it out. But not this time.

Step by fearful step, Finn drove Lars's horse back towards the road, nipping at his hindquarters. Aein drove her own horse forward, keeping the rope taut so Lars's mount knew which direction to go. The sound of the wolf snarling and barking, the screams and pants of the horse, the sound of Lars shouting at the animal to keep it fighting - Aein knew they would color her nightmares. Finally, half dragging the animal out of the bog, the horse was on the road. Its ears were pressed against the back of its head and its eyes were white with terror.

"Shhhh! Shhhh! Shhhh!" Aein whispered, trying to calm it.

Though its breath was heaving in its sides and exhaustion should have quieted it, it snapped and bit and kicked whenever she tried to get near it. She needed the rope and it was not cooperating.

Lars was sinking fast into the mud. Every step was making it worse. The weight of his armor was dragging him down. Finn leapt and paddled to his side, but they were both in terrible danger. Aein ran back to her saddle, throwing everything on the ground and rooting through the mess for something which might work. She grabbed her bow, laid down on the road, and reached it out to Lars, using it as an extension of her arm. He struggled and fought, half walking, half swimming, until the tips of his fingers reached the tip of the wood. The mud was up to his chest. Aein pulled with all her might. Lars wrapped his arm around Finn's torso and hauled him along. Aein cried out from the exertion, trying to keep focused on getting her friends to safety and not getting trampled by Lars's fool horse. Finally, Lars's fingertips touched the road.

Aein leaned out and wrapped her hands around Lars's wrists, ready to haul him out, but instead, he shouted at Finn. "Climb up my back!"

She could almost see the wheels in Finn's mind spin, wanting to protest against getting out first, but the wolf relented. Using Lars's back as a ladder, the wolf scrambled his way to safety.

And then Aein pulled with all her might. Lars already outweighed her, but with the armor and the weight of the muck, she feared she might go into the bog with him. She managed to get him to the road. He rested his elbows on the wooden slats. Lars swung one leg up, his toe catching the side, but couldn't hold it and fell again. He was exhausted and had to pause to gather his strength, but the mud would not let him. Finn paced back and forth, searching for some way to help.

Aein leaned down and wrapped her arms under Lars's armpits. He clung to her neck like a frightened child. She wriggled herself into a sitting position and leaned back, using all of Lars's weight to fall backwards. He came out of the muck with a squelching sound. They lay there for several moments, too exhausted to move. Finn came over and desperately began licking both their faces.

"I'm okay! I'm okay," protested Lars, pushing him

away. "Just give me a minute." Finn stepped back, shifting back and forth on his haunches as if ready to leap upon them again the moment they recovered.

Lars rolled off of Aein and fell beside her, his head resting on her arm as they caught their breath.

"Thanks," he said, opening up his eyes just long enough to look at her. He tapped his palm on his heart. "I thought I was done for."

Aein rolled over and hugged him tight. Her body was still shaking from terror. She thought she had lost him and in those moments it had felt like the whole world was going to end. She never wanted to let go of him ever again. "You're welcome," she whispered.

The moment was broken as Finn began to whine and bark. Aein turned her head to see what was disturbing him. "It's that damned bird again," she grunted.

"Maybe we should play dead," said Lars. "I feel like I could play dead very well right now."

Finn continued barking, the insistence in his voice becoming clearer.

Lars rolled onto his side, pausing for a moment on his hands and knees before pushing himself up to a standing position. He held out his hand to Aein. "Duty calls."

Aein struggled to her feet. She was encrusted in a layer of filthy brown. Finn and Lars were in even worse shape, covered from head to foot in muck.

Lars turned and rested a hand on Finn's shoulder. "Thank you," he said.

The wolf gave a whine.

Lars walked to his terrified horse and was able to unwind the rope from around its neck. "Idiot animal. Don't you know we execute soldiers who desert?" He removed a shirt from his bedroll and tied it over the animal's eyes like a mask. Immediately, it calmed down. He gave it an understanding slap on its shoulders. "Don't worry, my friend. I feel the same way. No one goes willingly into the swamp if they know what is in there."

As if to punctuate his words, a biting wind blew down the planks of the road. Aein tried to tell herself it was just because the temperature was cooler beneath the trees, but she couldn't shake the sense that something watched in the shadows. She shivered.

As they walked into the swamp, the fog was still present, but it did not wrap around them like it had in the past. Aein wondered what had distracted it. To generate fear seemed to be its only reason for existence.

Moss dripped from bare branches like spider webs. A layer of bright green algae covered the water, rippling sluggishly as it lapped the roots of the trees. They walked on and soon came to the clearing with the bush. Aein peered in. Though the bush was still there, there was no sign of anyone from the Haidra kingdom.

"Where is the guard?" she murmured to Lars.

He shook his head, as mystified as her. Finn crept beside them. The fur on his back was raised, but not aimed at anything in particular.

They continued on for hours. Aein stifled the urge to call out to see if anyone was there. She didn't want to attract unwanted attention. The tension was so thick, it made her want to run and hide like a mouse. Neither Lars nor Finn made a sound. Even their horses seemed to step lightly.

The road led to the campground where she and Lars had spent the first night, the night when he first transformed into a wolf and killed the guard. He had been trapped here the rest of the time, slowly going insane.

But while the fog had kept back from them during their journey, this time it blocked their way completely, cutting off the road like a curtain. Lars pulled his horse to a stop. He tugged at the neck of his armor as if the metal was cutting off his breath. Aein reached over and gripped his hand, asking silently if he was able to go on. Finn waited as Lars wrestled his feelings under control. Finally, he nodded and all three of them stepped into the mist.

At first it was just white and grey. Then came the sounds. The snuffling, breathing sounds. Then the noise of angry jaws snapping and biting. It was just a trick of the fog, she told herself.

"That was me..." Lars's voice cracked.

And then they were through. The campground sat before them, the wooden road gone as the land rose above the marshy waterline.

"They're dead," whispered Aein in horror. "They are all dead."

CHAPTER EIGHT

Aein choked back the bile as it rose in her throat. She needed to be strong for Lars, she told herself. She fixed on him, but as their eyes locked, she realized he was telling himself the same thing.

The campground was littered with bodies. Their heads were twisted on their necks and their stomachs had been ripped open by something with sharp claws. The doors had been ripped off the wooden sleeping shacks to get at the people inside. They had been dead for some time. The stench of the rot sat heavy in the air. Flies and maggots were making a meal of these guardsmen, these loyal people who had faithfully served Queen Gisla. They had not been killed by some wild animal for food, they had been killed for the joy of death.

Finn sat on his haunches, unable to stop himself, and lifted his muzzle to the sky, letting out a plaintive howl. He had known them all, Aein realized. He served with these men and women. He would have been the one to send them to this doom.

She ran forward and wrapped her arms around his body as he continued to cry in the only way his form would allow. She glanced up. Lars was picking his way through the carnage. He opened his hands and placed them against four evenly spaced slashes in the tree. He could not spread his fingers wide enough to fit in the marks. It was a monster who had done this, something so huge it could rip into the trunk of a tree with a swipe of its paw.

Aein thought of what Finn and Lars had been before they'd eaten the berries. They had been driven by this same instinct to destroy. Whatever did this was not just some animal, it was a creature of the swamp.

Lars tied the horses to a far tree, giving them enough lead so they could eat what they could of the sparse grass. Finn finally stopped howling. He leaned his whole weight against Aein, whimpering with every breath. Lars crouched down beside him. "We have to burn the bodies before the sun goes down," he said, his emotions masked beneath the stone surface of duty. "Bodies in the swamp have been known to rise."

She brushed back Finn's filthy mats of muddy fur. "I need you to find safe water for us to clean ourselves in. We will handle this," she promised.

Finn wobbled away, as if each step caused him pain.

"Come on," said Lars to Aein. "We have to do this."

They began gathering wood and got the pit started. Once the fire was crackling, there was no putting it off any longer. Aein and Lars, picking up and pulling what they could, drew the bodies to the fire. It had been so long since they died that some of the body parts fell off as they carried them. Aein had to stop to empty the contents of her stomach several times. The stench of charred, rotting, human flesh was one of the worst things she ever endured. Lars continued on with a grim stoicism. Here she thought she would need to be the one to lend him strength, and he was the one taking it most in stride.

Finn returned, but they did not acknowledge him until the last body was on the fire. The sun was hanging low in the sky by the time they were done.

Aein and Lars grabbed clean clothes from their packs and then followed Finn to a spring which they were both already very much aware was there. They just needed to give Finn a job while they handled his friends.

Aein and Lars stripped, helping each other out of their armor and all three of them dove into the pond. Between the muck from the bog and the filth Aein did not want to contemplate from the camp, the water was soon murky and brown. Aein kept an alert eye for creatures who might try to sneak up on them. By the time they were clean, it was almost time for the transformation. Aein climbed out of the water followed by Finn and Lars. They dressed in silence. None of them made a move to go back to the campground.

The shift came. It was a gentle ripple. One minute, Finn was in wolf form, and the next he was human. His eyes were full of tears, his face full of grief.

"Thank you for saving me in the bog," said Lars, coming forward and gripping Finn's arm. The man nodded his head in acceptance.

"We must decide what we need to do next," said Finn, his voice cracking. "What is your recommendation?"

Lars rubbed his hands through his wet, red hair. "That we set fire to this entire swamp and call it a day?"

Finn laughed a harsh, sad chuckle. "I shall be the first with a torch."

"We have to leave two here on the border," Lars stated. There was a resigned finality to his tone. He knew he was the best choice to stay. "If we don't, more of what caused this will come through. We have to hold the swamp—"

That was all they had time for. Just as Lars was about to continue his sentence, he faded. Frustration crossed his face before his emotions were lost behind his muzzle and fur.

Finn rested his hand upon Lars's powerful shoulder. "We shall hold the border," he promised. He directed Aein. "You will need to ride as quickly as possible to

Queen Gisla—"

Aein cut him off. "You mean you need to ride as quickly as possible to Queen Gisla."

The silence between them was charged with energy. Even the birds stopped singing. Finn turned back to Lars and asked, "Would you give us a minute?"

The wolf got up quickly, as if he wanted no part of this discussion. He trotted off towards the camp without pausing to look back.

When he was out of sight, Finn came back to Aein. "I cannot leave you here in the swamp," argued Finn.

"This swamp is a part of the land which I belong," Aein pointed out. "If a soldier from Lord Arnkell's stronghold shows up here and sees you, he'll kill you. No questions asked. It will be a sign of war and end whatever truce, uneasy as it might be, between Queen Gisla and Lord Arnkell. At least if I stay, there's a chance it might be someone I know and can talk some sense to them."

"That's not an option—" Finn began.

But Aein would not give. She held up her hand and ticked off the points on each of her fingers. "You are the only one who knew these men and women and you owe it to them to deliver this news to their families. You're the only one who knows what size an army needs to be brought back. You're the only one who can organize the troops. And finally..." Aein glanced away. A strange lump rose in her throat. "I cannot lead a war." She shrugged apologetically. "If I came across Lord Arnkell marching with a battalion of guards, I do not know if I could tell Queen Gisla's army to attack my old friends. Please don't make me kill my people until I absolutely have to."

Finn gripped her arms, pleading, "I cannot allow you to stay here. If I come back and find you slaughtered like that—"

"Finn, Lars needs me. You and he might be able to live because of the shift, but he needs me to help keep him sane. I am the only one who knew what he went through."

And then, without a word of warning, Finn bent down and pressed his lips against Aein's, his stubble rough around her mouth. His arms engulfed her, wrapping her so tight, she wasn't sure where her body ended and his began. She felt herself melting, the heat chasing away all the horrors of the swamp. The kiss was desperate and urgent. It devoured her whole. It was as if he needed to fit a lifetime of regrets and passion into that one moment. It was as if he didn't trust she would be there for him to ever touch again. When they parted, he rested his forehead against hers. "Don't you dare die on me. Don't you dare be the one I find in a heap, slaughtered by some monster because I wasn't fast enough getting back. Live."

Aein flung her arms around his neck and held him close, the thinness of her linen shirt allowing the heat of his body to seep into her skin, allowing the beating of his heart to play against hers. She pressed her lips to his temple so that her words would rumble in his bones. "I promise," she said. "I promise. Now, go."

Without another word, Finn turned and made his way back to the camp. She picked up the discarded armor and slowly made her way back, picking her way through the tree stumps and rocks. The fading twilight made it hard to see her way. Somewhere along the line Lars found her. She gripped onto his fur and let him guide her through. He made no indication that he saw what passed between her and Finn, but she was sure he could smell Finn all over her.

By the time they reached the camp, Finn had loaded up one of the horses with the few provisions he would need to get back to the Haidra kingdom. He turned back to Aein and Lars, that lapse of passion now hidden behind his duty. "You take care of her. I am leaving her in your care and will hold you responsible if anything happens." His eyes locked with Aein's and she knew his words were meant for her. "I will be back. I promise, I will be back. I will fly as quickly as my horse will let me and I will return."

Aein raised her hand in goodbye as he mounted and was gone, disappearing into the darkness. They stood there long after the sound of the hooves faded and the still silence returned to the swamp. Aein stared down at Lars as Finn's final words looped in her head. She tried to force back the memory of the time she had been the one on horseback, the time when she had been the one to leave the swamp. She had made the same promise not so long ago.

CHAPTER NINE

With night descending, there was nothing to do but sleep. Aein stepped towards the fire pit as if in a trance and then stopped. Fire could only do so much to cremate the dead. The pit was filled with bones, the bones of their slaughtered fellows. She could not force herself to stay here. Death hung in the air. The smell of the ash was infused in every inch of the cursed place. The fog was beginning to build just outside the circle of the camp, as if trying to figure out the perfect time to creep in. She could not face the horrors of what it might play in her mind tonight, especially when reality was even more terrifying. She went into one of the shacks and grabbed a lantern from inside.

"Come on," she said to Lars.

He whined, unsure of what she was proposing.

"I can't stay here," Aein explained, gripping one arm tightly around her waist to keep herself from shaking. "We'll come back tomorrow when I can face this. But there are too many ghosts. I can't. Not tonight."

He whined again and Aein could tell he thought she was foolish, but he followed her, nevertheless, as she took the horses' reins and led the animals out.

The swamp loomed before them and Aein was not sure if her unease was just the memories of what it once held or some form of actual malice that seemed to radiate from the darkness. The horses' hooves struck the wooden planked road. The fog was crawling out from beneath the drowned trees. Its white fingers crept towards them, lapping their legs, and tangling through their limbs.

There should have been the sound of birds or frogs, but the swamp was eerily quiet, as if everything was in hiding, smothered beneath a blanket of fear. And then there was a sound.

"Do you hear that?" Aein whispered to Lars. He glanced up at her with worried eyes, but continued walking.

The sound became louder. It was screams and cries. The heavy breath of the monsters. The last noises of the battalion as they had been slaughtered. The fog replaying their final moments so that Aein would know the fate waiting for her if she stayed.

But the fog had played this trick before, and this time, it just strengthened her resolve to not leave the border unprotected when more that caused this sort of destruction could get through.

"It is just the fog," Aein stated for her own benefit. Lars's body was rigid with tension. Aein would have stopped to comfort him, but with the lantern in one hand and the reins of the horses in the other, all she could do was lean over and whisper, "Remember to breathe."

He took in a great gulp of air and whined.

"You are not alone," Aein reminded him.

But then Lars looked straight out into the shadows of the trees and a growl replaced the whine.

"We are not alone, are we?" Aein asked, realizing the fog was hiding something out there beyond just sound and fear. She said a silent prayer that Finn had made his way out of the swamp, that she would not stumble and look down and see it was his body she had tripped over.

Lars raised his mouth to the sky and let out a warning howl. His voice quieted as he waited for a response. Something large and lumberous shuffled through the branches and reeds. She put down the lantern and ran to her saddle bags to pull out her arrows and bow, even as the horses danced around in circles. There was no place to tie them up.

"If you bolt," she swore at them, "I'll feed you to the darkness myself."

Holding her spare arrows with her draw hand, she loaded the first onto the string. She didn't know if there would be enough time to use it. She unbuttoned the flap which kept her mace strapped to her side.

Aein looked down at Lars and nodded that she was ready. "Drive it away."

At once, he was off, snarling and breathing heavy as he crashed into the waters of the swamp. There was a yip of pain, but no sounds of struggle. She hoped maybe he just landed on a sharp rock as opposed to something with claws and fangs.

But then she heard the fight. There was a roar which shook the ground and the sound of something falling, which seemed as big as a tree. Whatever it was cried out in anger. The creature was getting closer. She aimed her arrow in the direction of the noise, trying to ignore the shooting pain from her old injury, trying to steady the shake of her weak arms.

Suddenly, the monster came into view.

It had the shape of a man, but seemed as tall as a mountain. He had one eye, set in the middle of his forehead. He was naked but covered in a thick pelt of his own fur. Lars was unable to pierce his hide, even with his massive jaws.

A cyclops. Aein swore.

She had been warned of these creatures when she began training. They were carnivores and happy to feast upon whatever meat they could crush in their fists. He most likely had been tracking them from the moment they stepped outside of the camp. Cyclops were not supposed to travel this close to the border. They stayed deeper in the swamp. Their hides were as tough as stone and they had few weaknesses - the tendon between their ankle and their single eye.

Aein pulled back and released her arrow. Her aim was off after so long without practice. The cyclops had been distracted, but not enough to ignore a projectile flying towards his only source of vision. He ducked, and with a sweep of his hand flung Lars into a rock with a sickening crunch. But there was no time for Aein to worry about him. The cyclops leaned forward and let out another mighty roar. She did not pause. She placed another arrow on the string and let it loose, praying that this one would fly true. The creature swatted it aside and kept coming towards her.

Aein pulled back another arrow and this one grazed his face. The monster was so close. She didn't know whether to keep firing her arrows or to cast her bow aside. She foolishly left her axe in her bedroll. Her blunt mace would be useless against him. But then Lars was back. Relief flooded through her as he flung himself upon the creature's tendon. The cyclops was off balance as he tried to shake and kick Lars off. He was distracted enough that he did not notice as Aein let her final arrow fly and it struck him through the white of his eye. Howling with pain, he stumbled off into the swamp, Lars fast upon his heels, nipping and biting and chasing him far away.

The silence he left behind was deafening. She collapsed onto the road. It felt like she had run a thousand miles. Though she had seen battle and slaughter, it was as if the swamp amplified her fear, amplified the danger to terrifying levels. She held out her fingers and they were trembling. She placed them upon her heart and was almost able to feel its pounding through her heavy breastplate.

Lars hauled himself out of the water. Panting, he sat down and pressed against her, as if the only payment he needed for all that he had done was an approving word, which she was happy to give.

"Thank you," she said as she ruffled his fur. "I have never heard of a cyclops so near the edge of the swamp before." She left unsaid that she worried what else might be waiting for them. As the adrenaline faded away, bone numbing exhaustion took its place. "We had better be going or I am going to fall asleep right here."

The horses had not fled and Aein wearily grabbed their reins. As they moved forward, each footstep seemed to hide a crackling twig, every shadow seemed to have fangs. Finally, they reached the entrance to the clearing which hid the sacred bush. As she stepped into the glen, it was as if all the horrors of the day were gone. There was a peace here, some sort of barrier from the rest of the swamp. She placed the lantern with its flickering light upon the ground and removed the saddles and supplies from the horses.

She took out her bedroll and placed it upon the ground. The night was cold. The air was damp. She knew she should dig a fire pit and get a flame going, but the thought was too much. She climbed in and hoped she would not freeze to death.

As if he could read her mind, Lars came over and climbed beneath the blanket with her. He was filthy and smelled of wet dog, but he radiated heat. She wrapped her body around his and burrowed her face into the soft warmth of his fur.

Before she drifted off, she almost began to laugh hysterically. This had only been the first day.

CHAPTER TEN

Aein's eyes opened and she realized Lars had shifted. She was not spooned around the body of a werewolf, but instead, around the body of her best friend. She started to pull back, but his hands took her wrists and he gently pulled her back into place.

"Stay," he whispered.

It was cold outside and he was warm, so she did.

Lars stroked her arm. "So what shall we do today?" he asked.

Aein pressed her cheek against his back. "Besides finding out what else is waiting in the fog to kill us?" replied Aein. She felt Lars sigh, knowing that their safe cocoon would have to be abandoned.

"Let's not think about all that death stuff until later," he said.

She groaned and sat up.

"Come back," he whined.

"No," said Aein, standing up. Her bones creaked and popped from sleeping on the ground. Her injuries ached. She ticked off all the necessaries for their survival. "We need to gather firewood. Hunt for some food so we're not eating all our stores. Go back to the camp and see if we can repair it enough to stay there. If we lead something to this glen…" Their precious bush was now visible in the daylight. It was still in hibernation without a single sign of bloom. She was terrified to leave it unguarded, but terrified their presence might guide something to it. She felt like a bird trying to trick a predator away from a nest of defenseless chicks. She sighed. "We are a choice menu item for practically every creature here and we can't afford some stumbling cyclops to accidentally step on the bush while he tries to make us lunch."

Lars rolled onto his back and laced his fingers behind his head in resignation. "You're right."

"How are we supposed to protect the entire border just by ourselves, Lars?" Aein asked as the memory of last night's battle crashed back into her thoughts. "This is a suicide mission."

"Yes," he said. "Every tour on the border is."

She pointed her finger at him. "You are not helping."

He sat up and laid it out for her. "We are out-manned, out-maneuvered, and completely about to die. Welcome to the guard."

"Do you think there is anyone left?" asked Aein, quietly.

The camp was the central hub for the Arnkell army. They met there with their replacements and traveled out to the territory they would be protecting. There was only one road going in and out, so everyone leaving would have to pass through. She hoped there was a chance that someone could still be out there wandering the border.

"Not after this much time," said Lars. "You and I were the last to be deployed to this area. Anyone serving a tour would have long since gone home."

Aein kicked the ground. The realization was sickening. No one came home after Lars ate the mushrooms. And now she understood that he, in werewolf form, was the reason. She had not understood viscerally why he hated his shift so much, but did now. The massacre they found last night was something he woke up to every morning. He made the mistake of holding his post. How many people had died because he would not leave? He had stayed in the camp, thinking he was creating a safe haven, when in fact, any of their fellow guardsmen who came walked into their own death.

"I don't want to stay in the camp," Aein blurted out.

"Me, neither," he replied. "We need to repair it, in case help comes. But we won't stay."

The wind began blowing through the trees and Aein shivered. It was not from the cold. "Let's go now. I want to make sure we are out of there before nightfall."

Lars stood and rolled up their wool blanket. They helped each other put their armor on. Aein wondered if she should start sleeping in the metal plate. Lars held out the reins of her horse to Aein, but she did not mount. Instead, she walked the horse out of the clearing. Immediately the fog enveloped them.

"It is like it was waiting for us," Aein hissed with frustration as the sounds of battle surrounded her again.

"It was," replied Lars.

Aein walked over to her pack and drew out her axe. She held it loose by her side.

"Good thinking," said Lars. "I wouldn't know something was about to attack us unless it had its claws through my neck." The metal rang against the scabbard as Lars unsheathed his sword.

Then another gust rattled through the trees, but with it, the fog thickened and Lars disappeared into the white.

"I cannot see you," said Aein, "even though I know you are walking just feet away from me."

"Keep talking. I am going to reach out to you," said Lars. "Try not to cut off my hand."

Aein was glad he gave her warning, because it took all her strength not to strike as his phantom fingers broke through the mist and grabbed at her.

"That is you, correct?" she asked. "Not some undead

creature who decided to take advantage?"

"You should be so lucky," Lars replied.

They walked in silence, feeling the path with their feet. Suddenly, she saw a shape, a silhouette in the fog.

"Hello?" she called.

"What do you see, Aein?" Lars asked.

"It's…" her breath caught in her throat. A lump formed, threatening to spill tears from her eyes. "Cook Bolstad?" she called again.

"It's not him, Aein," Lars stated.

The sound of Lars's voice was unwelcome. His words harsh and unkind in her ears. She knew the man that the shadow belonged to. It was Cook Bolstad. It was him. He was alive.

"Aein?" Cook Bolstad replied back.

She loosened her fingers from Lars, but he wouldn't let go. She leaned towards Cook Bolstad, trying to tear away. She thought about hacking Lars's arm off if he didn't let her run to her friend. Cook Bolstad was there. Right there. He was dead, but now he was not and she didn't understand why Lars wouldn't let her go to him.

"It is not him!" Lars shouted.

"Let me go!" Aein screamed.

The flat of Lars's sword struck the side of her metal helmet. The noise rang in her ears like a bell. Immediately she stopped and realized the shadow was gone. "Where is he?" she whispered.

"It was a phantom, Aein," Lars replied, squeezing her hand.

The fog began to lift and Lars appeared. There was so much understanding sadness in his eyes. "It is just the swamp playing tricks on you."

At once, the longing to run towards a shadow seemed ridiculous. The belief it was a living man whom she knew was dead made no sense.

Lars did not move. He brushed back a lock of her blonde hair and gently guided her back to reality. "When I was here before, I saw these figures all the time. Fallen friends. Family that was gone. I chased one once right into a bog. If it had not been sunset and if I had not transformed into a werewolf just moments later, I would have died. It is the swamp trying to kill you, Aein. It is the swamp trying to ingest your power."

It became difficult for Aein to breathe. "It was waiting for me. It knew exactly what I needed in order to be lured away." She looked at Lars. "The swamp knew..."

Aein wet her lips, which were suddenly dry though her palms were sweaty, the panic of their situation beginning to build.

Lars sheathed his sword and took Aein's axe from her limp hand, placing it into her holster for her. He wrapped her up in his arms, resting his head against the top of hers. "It always does," he said. "And it will get worse."

"Lars, how will we survive these two months?" she asked, no longer able to pretend to be the brave soldier she was supposed to be. "How?"

His body softened against hers. "The good news is that with two people here, we can watch out for each other," said Lars, his voice rumbling deep inside of her. "We can keep the swamp from overtaking us. Be my eyes and ears, Aein. And I'll be yours."

What would she have done without him? Die, she realized. She gazed up at her tall, gangly, red-haired friend, the man who had been there for her since the beginning. How could she have left him in the swamp for so long? How could she have left him to face all of this on his own, even if he had been the perpetrator of the horrors he had seen? He survived it. And now, he was helping her to survive. If it hadn't been for him, if it hadn't been for his terrible ordeal, she would be dead now. He let her cling to him until the fear faded. He gave her this moment to rest.

And then she realized her vulnerability actually gave him strength, gave him something to think about besides his own fear. She had grown up needing to be so hard, needing to protect herself after her parents died. The only person who looked out for her was Cook Bolstad until she met Lars, and she had thought she needed to stay unbreakable. But by allowing Lars to see her broken and support her, it didn't give him room to think about his own troubles.

Aein never thought of that before, that somehow allowing someone to give her strength gave them strength.

"Shh. We will get through this," he murmured. "Even if it is just you and me, we will get through this."

And Aein was happy to give him all the strength he needed.

CHAPTER ELEVEN

They returned to the campground and set about the task of making it habitable again, spending most of the day in silence. Lars found a snake for them to eat, but game was scarce. They cleared away the last ashes of the bodies, scattering them to the wind, and tried to wash the blood from the walls.

"It is stained," said Aein, pushing back the sweat from her forehead with the back of her hand. "We'll have to replace the wood."

Lars came over and examined her handiwork. "Or we could stain the wood to match."

"I am not opening a vein to paint a shack," Aein replied, earning a smile from him.

"A true soldier would give her blood, sweat, and tears for the needs of her people."

"You are not people."

"There are other people who will come here that will be people," he ribbed.

Aein couldn't help laughing.

"I was thinking more along the lines of finding some berries…" he said.

"Not berries…" Aein replied with a groan.

"...or something else which causes stains," added Lars, holding up his hands in protest.

Aein pursed her lips. "It might work."

"It'll work better than trying to hack down a bunch of trees and rebuild every structure in this camp."

"You've got something better to do?" she asked.

"I can think of about twenty different things."

"Name one."

He squinted down at her good-natured challenge, and his eyes said that at least nineteen of those things would involve her. But instead he said, "Eat that delicious snake I so bravely caught for us."

He walked back to the fire and turned the snake on its spit. Aein came over. "I have seen leather thongs with more meat on them."

"I should know better than to cook for the kitchen's favorite apprentice," retorted Lars.

"You should," she replied, giving him a bump with her shoulder.

Suddenly, she stopped. She realized all of the sounds in the swamp had stopped. She reached towards her belt, realizing that she had left her axe by the shack.

"What is it?" said Lars.

The answer came from the forest as twenty men stepped into the camp, arrows and weapons drawn.

"I believe we might be 'it'," said the leader of the group.

It was soldiers from the Arnkell stronghold. They wore the simple green and yellow leather armor of their old home. Aein even recognized their leader, a lower soldier named Paske. He was a good man when sober, but had a habit of smashing up taverns when he was not. He used to spend as much time under disciplinary action as he did doing his actual job. But his fists were solid and Lord Arknell always valued him when someone needed roughing up. From the paint on his shoulder, it seems Paske had been elevated in rank since the war began. His bald head was filthy with grime and sweat. His entire company was gaunt and their eyes haunted. She could tell they had not had enough to eat. What better way to beat the drums of war than to tell your people all the food they could want was just one kingdom over? With just a modest invasion, it could all be theirs for the taking. Hunger drove people to desperate actions.

"Paske! Friends from Lord Arnkell's stronghold!" Aein exclaimed, trying to overcome the tension with a friendly greeting. But as she stepped forward to take the leader's hand, the entire group raised their weapons.

"We remember what you are, Aein," the man spat. "And you, too, Lars. Werewolf loving traitors."

From the weapons they carried and lack of supplies, it did not seem like they were here to take over the post. "You have it all wrong," Aein replied, her mind working to diffuse the situation. "Please, come share what food we have. Sit and take advantage of our hospitality and let us talk."

"Hospitality?" Paske turned to his friends and laughed. It was an ugly sound. "And why would a traitorous kitchen wench like you be so anxious to share her 'hospitality' with the people she left to die? Why are you two in the wrong end of the swamp?" he asked. "Did that general, oh what was his name... that fellow who was riding hell-for-leather to the Haidra kingdom just yesterday... Finn? Did he leave you here to die?"

Fearfully, Aein locked eyes with Lars. How did they know about Finn? Did they capture him? Did they kill him?

"...and now you hope you can wheedle your way back into our good graces by offering us a snake?" the man continued.

Lars stepped forward, holding out his hands in peace. "I swear we are only here to help. The border must always have two people guarding the line," he said. "There are monsters coming through—"

Paske cut him off. "The only monster we've seen is

that bitch-queen sitting on the throne of the Haidra kingdom. I use the term 'bitch' as a technical term." He scratched his crotch and laughed. "We know she turns into a dog every night."

"Whatever is happening between the Haidra kingdom and the Arnkell land is unimportant," said Aein, trying to calm everyone down. "The only thing that is important is holding the swamp. This border was left unprotected. Terrible things are getting through."

"Yeah, I'd say two terrible things got through all right and it is about time we took care of that." The man barked at one of his men. "Harness them."

"What?" asked Aein in confusion.

"We don't know if you're going to turn into bitey little dogs come sundown and I'd prefer not to take any chances, if you don't mind."

The other man stepped forward with two silver harnesses. He threw them at Aein and Lars's feet. Aein felt Lars shiver. The pain from the silver when he shifted would keep him in check and make it impossible for him to do anything but sit very still once twilight came.

"What are you going to do to us?" Aein asked.

"We're going to take you back to Lord Arnkell's stronghold and give you a chance to visit your old friend in a comfortable cell."

So they had caught Finn, Aein thought. There wasn't anything to be done now. Perhaps once night came and the guards went to sleep, Aein and Lars might have a chance to escape and get to the stronghold to free Finn.

"You're making a grave mistake," said Lars, reaching for the harness.

"Just put it on and I'll tell you if I've made a grave mistake," he replied.

Aein and Lars slipped their arms through the harnesses. Aein turned her back to Lars so that he could buckle the silver buckle. When he turned his back for her to do the same, she whispered a promise in his ear. "I will get you out of this," she said.

"No talking!" shouted the man. He was distracted by the gashes in the trees. "What's this from?" he asked.

"That's what we were trying to tell you," said Aein. "That's why we are here."

"Probably just a bear," Paske dismissed, but his fingers kept tracing the marks.

"There are no bears in the swamp," Lars replied.

"You don't know that," he said. But, for all his faults, Paske was not an idiot. Aein saw a flash across his face as he realized they might not have been lying outright. He directed his men. "Get a good look around. Make sure there's nothing hiding in the shadows, would you?" He then saw the stains on the wood. He peered closer and squinted. "This doesn't look natural."

"There were a lot of good men and women who died here," Aein informed him.

"Our people?"

"No, but good people nevertheless."

"How many?"

"All of them."

Paske hesitated, but then sniffed. "Served them right." He balled his fists and took a wide stance. "Teach them to be in places they shouldn't be. Should have kept to their own portion of the swamp."

"We are just trying to help!" said Aein, unable to keep the frustration out of her voice.

Paske lifted his arm to hit her across the face with the back of his hand but stopped himself. "Just give me a reason..." he threatened. But Aein could tell the real reason he stopped was the possibility she was telling the truth.

The truth decided to come overhead with a screeching cry.

Before he could warn his party to arm themselves, a body struck the ground in front of them. It was one of his soldiers. Only his head had been turned on his neck.

"What fresh hell...?" Paske whispered, stepping forward. He glared at Aein, looking for somewhere to aim his confusion and rage. "What did this?"

Aein scanned overhead, but the fog had come in and shrouded the sky, masking out even the sun.

And then another body dropped, hitting the ground beside them.

"ARM YOURSELF!" Paske cried in terror.

Aein ran to grab her weapon but he pointed his sword at her. "Not you! You stay here where I can see you."

"Let me help you!" she shouted.

"Let you slit my throat while I'm trying to defeat this...thing? Is that what you mean? Get back!"

Aein walked to Lars and gripped his hand. They didn't stand a chance. She had seen what it had done to their troops. She had cleared the bodies herself. Another soldier's corpse struck the ground, his stomach opened by sharp claws. She pressed her forehead into Lars's shoulder. "I am so sorry," she said to him. "I am sorry I could not tell you that I love you."

Her words yanked him away from the terror of the moment, his face a mixture of shock and surprise just as the sun struck the horizon.

"No..." he whispered, looking down at his hands as they began to change.

"One minute," she whispered aloud as she scanned the skies. One minute before she would be completely alone, before the only person on her side shifted and was trapped in the body of a wolf. "Oh dear gods..."

Lars limped to the body of the fallen soldier and picked up his sword. Every movement seemed to cause him agony as the silver harness pressed into his changing body. He pointed the tip of the sword at the sky, fighting the change. It seemed as if it was causing him agony to hold onto his human form. "I won't leave you, Aein!" he shouted. But then, he shifted, unable to stop it any longer, unable to hold the sword.

Aein watched as the man who held them captive didn't know whether to kill Lars or the monster first. She heard the creature whizzing through the trees, the sound of flapping and wings in the air. One moment it sounded directly in front of her. The next, on the other side of the clearing. Aein ran and picked up the sword Lars dropped. It was a two-handed blade, too heavy for her to lift. Lars was writhing on the ground, the silver harness burning through his fur.

And then, Paske was gone, lifted up into the sky and into the fog. And then he dropped, his neck broken, his eyes vacant and lifeless.

He had a dagger at his side and Aein scrambled over, her terrified fingers trembling and slipping as she tried to undo the buckle holding it in place.

Lars began barking. It was a warning cry. He ran and leaped, striking something solid.

And just as her fingers grabbed the dagger, the creature had her by the shoulders and was hauling her up.

Aein lifted her head to figure out what captured her. It appeared to be a winged woman with wild hair and rows of sharp teeth. Her eyes were red and her claws were hooked. She looked like what would have happened if a person had tried to shift into a dragon form, but had gotten caught halfway. Her skin was yellow and scaly. Her hair was wild and the color of an apple.

"Harpy!" Aein screamed, hoping anyone who was still alive could hear her warning. She saw the harpy's hooked claws reach down for her neck to snap her in two. Everything slowed and Aein felt like she was seeing the whole world through a tunnel. Aein was not going to die without a fight. Aein put the knife between her teeth, grabbed onto the harpy's ankles and flung her own legs upward. She wrapped her feet around the harpy's neck, and used her weight to fling the harpy upside-down.

The harpy's legs let go of Aein's shoulders and now tried to scratch Aein like a cat disembowels its prey. The harpy's claws ripped at Aein's armor, but when they touched the silver harness, she hissed and pulled back. They were a ball of fists and claws rolling in the sky. Aein twisted her body around so that she was sitting on the harpy's shoulders. The creature dove and bucked, trying to knock Aein off. Aein took the silver dagger and began stabbing wildly, releasing the fury she had built up over months. With a gurgling cry, the creature fell, clawing at the air.

Aein braced herself as the earth grew closer. The harpy's wings were outstretched as she tried with one last gasp to escape the inevitable. But Aein forced the harpy's body to the ground first and used the creature to cushion her own fall. She rolled off as they hit, feeling as if a horse kicked her in the chest. She needed to close her eyes... just for a moment... The darkness was so soft... so welcoming...

She opened her eyes and the fog had rolled in. The world was nothing but dim and gray, illuminated by only the flicker of the campfire. She wondered how Lars lit the flames with his wolf paws. She saw the campgrounds were filled with sleeping shapes tucked into their bedrolls. Something told her not to call out, not to wake them.

It was as if they were inside of a gigantic bubble. Outside the protection of their dome was a world of nothing but white and fog. Even the trees were gone. She realized Finn was sitting upon a log by the fire. His eyes scanned the skies overhead. There was a vague memory that he should be somewhere else. A winged shape flew by, but did not venture any closer. Finn did not acknowledge her and she knew to leave him alone.

She heard footsteps coming towards her and she sat up in her bedroll. A figure came out of the fog.

"No..." she whispered.

It was Cook Bolstad, the man who raised her, the man responsible for making her poison her own people.

"You're dead," she said, trying to remind herself. Perhaps he had not died. Perhaps he had been here all along, looking for her,

looking for the cure. Perhaps it had been nothing but some terrible mistake.

But then he reached out for her and she could see he was not alive. His face was deathly pale, his hands were bony and skeletal. When he opened his mouth, he began to fall apart.

"I did it for you..." he whispered, his voice carried to her on the edge of a breeze. "Seek me, Aein... Find me... I did it for you..."

Then the last of his flesh crumbled away, leaving behind the shape of a hawk who took to the skies and flew away.

CHAPTER TWELVE

"Aein?" said a soft voice.

Aein's eyes flew open.

It had just been a nightmare. Her heart pounded like it might explode out of her chest. She had to hold on to the dream. Cook Bolstad traveled from beyond the grave to send her a message. It was fading. What did he tell her? He told her to find him. How could she find him? He was dead. He died in the stronghold, slaughtered in the kitchen, burned by Queen Gisla as they tried to ensure those who were dead would stay dead.

"Aein?" said the voice again.

Lars was kneeling beside her. The sun was up and light filled the sky. They were still in the camp, but Finn was not by the fire, shapes of sleeping figures were not tucked into their bedrolls. It was just her and Lars. The pain in her head thumped and every inch of her body felt like it had been horsewhipped.

"Where is everyone?" she asked, wetting her lips and wincing.

"Dead," he said. "Dead or gone. No one came back after you killed that thing." He motioned to the harpy's body lying beside the fire. Aein noted he had torn off its head.

"Precautionary measure or anger management?" Aein asked.

"Both."

"Good," murmured Aein.

Lars put his arm behind Aein's shoulders and shifted her into a sitting position. Her ribs ached. Nothing felt broken, but it hurt. Lars gazed into her eyes. "Your pupils seem to be the same size, so I am afraid you cannot blame anything on hitting your head."

"There goes my best excuse," said Aein.

He planted a relieved kiss on her forehead. "You scared me when you wouldn't wake up."

She allowed Lars to help her to her feet. She grunted, pausing a moment to rest her hands on her thighs as she caught a few deep breaths. The rush of blood made her woozy. "Remind me to stop being the hero, would you?"

"Stop being the hero."

"Done," she said as she stood up.

Lars was fiddling nervously with his silver harness as he watched her. The buckles were constructed in such a way that he could not remove it by himself.

"Want me to help you get that off?" she asked.

"You may remove any articles of my clothing you see fit," he replied.

She ruffled his hair and turned him around. "This will be quite enough for the moment," she said. Her fingers felt like she was moving them through mud and they would not work the way she wanted them to. "Kind of a shame. My harness ended up saving me."

"Really?" he asked, glancing at the harpy's corpse as if she might pipe up to confirm Aein's claim.

With no comment from the dead body, Aein continued. "The harpy couldn't touch it and it was a silver blade which let me cut its throat."

The harness slid off of Lars's shoulders. He let it drop to the ground and stretched out his chest and arms. "Ye gods it feels good to get out of that thing. I think I'll take my chances with the harpy."

"Did it hurt you?" Aein asked.

Lars answered with a small nod. He pulled back the edge of his shirt. There were great red welts weeping angrily on his skin. "Whenever I moved and it got passed the fur, it burned," he said. "I have no idea how they kept those wild werewolves harnessed."

"Maybe they don't feel it as much," said Aein.

"Better not to feel it at all," said Lars with finality, picking up the harness and throwing it into the swamp. It dropped into the water with a splash.

"Do you think they have Finn held in one of those?" Aein asked.

The ripples of where the silver landed spread out, as if with the horror of what her question meant.

"They must have been lying," said Lars. "He would never have allowed himself to be caught."

"So you're saying you think he is dead?"

Lars rubbed his hands through the waves of his dark auburn hair. "He can't be dead."

"I dreamed of him last night," said Aein. Her words came as if from another world. "He was sitting by a fire, scanning the skies for more harpies. He was here. Protecting us. And then Cook Bolstad came to me and told me to find him."

"It was just a dream, Aein."

"But what if it wasn't?" She looked at Lars. "What if they are both ghosts who came to visit me last night when I was so close to death?"

Lars did not say anything. He dug his shoe into the dirt. "I couldn't help you," he said. "You were lying there and I tried to wake you. I stayed with you all night keeping you warm, but I couldn't help you because of these paws." He held up his hands and gazed at them as if they had betrayed him. "I was so scared that you were going to die."

"Well, it looks like death won't have me," she replied.

Finn looked down at the ground and shifted uncomfortably. "Did you mean it?" he asked.

"Did I mean what?"

"Did you mean it when you said you loved me?"

The moment came rushing back Aein, the moment she had stood there, seeing death coming. She realized that if life was going to end, there was one thing she needed to say to Lars.

"Of course I meant it," Aein replied. Her cheeks burned. But she didn't know if it was what she wanted or needed right now. Lars had come to her that night of the battle, come to her in her room and begged her to run away with him. They had never discussed it since. She knew he had feelings for her. She didn't know how much was her, and how much was them just trying to survive and being the only ones who understood one another.

Lars took her hand, reading the conflict playing across her face. "Is the reason you can't love me because I'm a wolf?"

"No," she said, horrified he thought that at all. "No!"

"As soon as that berry bush blooms, I am going to eat them until this shift goes away. Don't worry," he tried to reassure her. "I will not be a monster forever."

"You are not a monster!" Aein hated that he hated this part of himself so much, hated that he saw this change as a curse. "We would have been dead if it hadn't been for your shift. The cyclops? Those spies on the road?"

"You see how well I helped. Lord Arnkell had people practically waiting here for us."

Aein stopped him. "Lars, you are perfect just the way you are. You have saved my life more times than I can count. But I almost died. Finn is rotting in a cell somewhere. We have a war to fight. This thing between us? The timing is just not..."

"Don't you see, Aein? This is our life. This is always the timing. It will never get better. When I saw you there dying, when I was powerless to do anything to stop it... I promised myself that if you woke, I would talk to you about this because we may never have a chance again. We are trapped here in the swamp and the reality is that at any moment a harpy could swoop down and end us. We may both be killed by some creature here or our old countrymen there and then it will be too late. I love you, Aein. And you said yesterday, when you were faced with death, you said that you loved me, too."

She thought back to the words which had come out of her lips. Lars was so good to her. He needed her. She was important to his life and sanity. She stepped forward, resting her cheek against his chest. It felt so good to just rest. To hold someone close. To be held. "I know what I said," she replied.

"And did you mean it?"

She lifted her face and gazed into Lars's soft, green eyes. "I could never lie to you," she said.

And he leaned down and kissed her.

CHAPTER THIRTEEN

They were hushed as they put their gear on their horses. Aein smiled at Lars shyly. Though it should not have made such a difference to have finally admitted their feelings, somehow it did. She still wasn't sure if it was good or bad. There was a part of her that mourned the loss of the friendship they had before. It was so uncomplicated. So fun. Now, there was so much more. But she knew she loved him. He had been there for her. He made her laugh. He needed her desperately. That had to be love, didn't it?

"Never thought I'd be putting on these old colors again," said Lars, fastening his belt.

They had decided to dress in the leather uniforms of the soldiers who had fallen. As repulsive as it was to take clothes off the dead, off people they had once known, they were going into Lord Arnkell's land and their own uniforms would stand out like a light in a mine. Their metal armor, their indigo shirts, it was nothing like the crude leathers the Arnkell people were used to seeing.

Lars came over and held her stirrup for her as she climbed onto her horse. Her body was not happy about getting into the saddle after her fight with the harpy. If it wasn't for the fact Finn might be dying and they were the only ones that knew he had been captured, she would have voted to stay in the cursed camp, monsters or not.

Lars's face broke into a huge, goofy smile as he looked at her. Her heart could not help but soften. She touched his cheek and then leaned forward in her saddle to give him one final soft kiss before they got on their way.

"Thank you," he said, as if she had given him the biggest gift in the world. He walked to his horse with a whistle on his lips and leapt up into the saddle. "Ready?" he asked.

Aein glanced back. "It will be good to see our old home again," she admitted. Then images of the past days flashed through her mind and she clarified, "Actually, it doesn't matter where we're off to. It will be good not to be here. Let's go."

They clicked their heels and the horses headed towards the exit of the swamp. For whatever reason, the fog left them alone. Perhaps the carnage had finally sated its appetite.

She had a hard time keeping her horse reined in. He was so excited to be leaving, he kept trying to take his head and run. Though the swamp was playing nice, she did not want to trigger a chase instinct in some predator they had not spotted. She was more than a little unnerved to see a hawk sitting on one of the branches watching them with a steady gaze. She wished Finn was there to let them know if it was bird or shifter.

They traveled for two weeks pushing their horses to the brink of exhaustion. Every moment they delayed was a moment which might cost Finn his life. They only paused when the highest tower of the Arnkell stronghold appeared over the tips of the trees.

Lars shivered and tightened his cloak around his body. "Welcome home."

Aein realized she was gripping the reins so tight her knuckles had turned white. It was strange to finally make the journey with Lars. If she had not accidentally turned him into a werewolf, they would have enjoyed catching this sight together months ago. Instead, her chest felt tight and it seemed hard to catch her breath. She was on this road before some of the worst moments of her life - her disgrace in the court after abandoning Lars on the border, her return to find Cook Bolstad dead. It felt as if she took another step forward, everything would happen again. Or, more frighteningly, something even worse.

A peasant passed by dressed in coarse rags. Upon her back she carried a bundle of switches taller than she was high. The old woman's misery spoke in her hunched shoulders and shuffling feet. Aein willed herself to memorize the woman's face. She told herself that as long as Lord Arnkell was allowed to continue in his war, this ancient grandmother would suffer. She had taken an oath as a guard of the Arnkell land to protect the people. She had not known at the time it would mean protecting them from their own master. To shy away because of her own fears and memories would mean she had failed her duty. Aein focused back on the tower. Her friend was trapped inside. She tried not to think of what they had been doing to Finn these two weeks. She tried to imagine him safe and whole, kept strong by the knowledge she would come. Aein and Lars could not fail him. They could not.

As if reading her mind, Lars asked quietly, "What do you think Queen Gisla will do if we have to tell her we lost Finn?"

Aein thought back to the way Queen Gisla looked at Finn. It was the look she saw on Lars's face. She thought about what Lars would do if Lord Arnkell ever killed her. "I believe Queen Gisla will slaughter every man, woman, and child in this land," said Aein with certainty. "We must make sure that does not happen."

"I wish we had a better plan."

"Me, too," Aein said.

They tapped their horses' sides and guided them into

the forest. They had decided to use the hidden entrance to the stronghold, the same one Aein used once before when she and Finn sneaked in. It was hidden by the side of a cave. Most anyone seeking shelter would head for the rocks and not give a second glance to a plain flagstone covered in leaves.

The entrance had not changed a bit, which was encouraging. In silence, they dismounted and ground-hitched the horses. Aein lifted up the stone. The staircase leading into the lower cavern was pitch black and, unfortunately, Aein and Finn had carried the lantern to the other end the last time they had used this entrance.

Aein walked over to her pack. She had a cow horn with the side cut out of it. Melted into the tip was a precious candle. It had never been meant for long term use, just enough in case they were in trouble. She believed this qualified. She just needed it to burn long enough to guide them through the cavern. Once they got in and freed Finn, he would be in wolf form and, if the gods were willing, he could lead them back through the dark.

Lars pulled out the flint from his saddle bag and was able to catch a few sparks on the wick. "We need to move fast," he said, discouraged by the amount of wax in the horn.

They dove into the caverns. The single candle eked out just enough light to guide them. Water dripped in the distance. Aein was happy to see that her old footprints from the previous trip were still undisturbed in the dirt. The exit seemed so much farther away than before, Aein thought, but finally they saw the first door. It was wide open, just as it had been left the last time Aein and Finn had been here. Behind it were four more doors, each untouched. A wave of relief engulfed Aein. Closing up this secret entrance seemed to have been forgotten in the chaos of the war. Lord Arnkell probably did not even know she was aware of it.

At the final door, Lars drew his sword. Aein blew the

light out and they were plunged into darkness except for a crack around the edge of the door. Blindly, Aein put her hand on the handle and pulled it open, trying to move the heavy wood slowly enough that the hinges did not give them away. The thick tapestry hanging in front of the doorway gave them a few more moments of privacy. She listened and there was no sound. She turned to Lars and waved for him to follow. She pushed back the edge of the fabric.

Standing there was Lord Arnkell and twenty of his soldiers.

"Welcome home, Aein," he replied with a smile. "We've been expecting you."

CHAPTER FOURTEEN

"Run," she whispered to Lars. But it was too late. A guard seized her by the arm and threw her to the ground, pressing his foot painfully into the back of her neck. She rolled her eyes to the side and saw they had forced Lars to the ground, too, pinning his elbows behind him. His blade lay uselessly beside him. The remaining soldiers held their swords at the ready to run them through if they tried to break away.

Lord Arnkell was leaner, his shorn brown hair was longer, but otherwise he had not changed. His square, chiseled jaw twitched as he looked at them with a mixture of contempt and amusement. His soft, leather-soled shoes barely made a sound as he walked towards Aein. He was always quiet before he struck. He wrapped his massive, calloused hand in her hair, and yanked her to her knees. He brought his face so close, she could smell the musky scent of his body, a scent she had found intoxicating when she worked as a kitchen wench. Now it turned her stomach.

He ran his finger across her cheek possessively. "And how is my favorite little traitor?" Aein tried to pull away, but he grabbed her face and brought her around until she was staring into his flat, brown eyes. "Now, now. Isn't this what you always wanted? The undivided attention of your lord and master?"

She said nothing, but let the rage and hatred burn within her. She was glad he was being cruel. It distracted her from the terror of what was to come. She glanced at the other soldiers, the men and women she had served with. She wondered how these fools could stand beside this man, the one man responsible for all of their suffering, and follow him like he was some sort of savior.

"Take these two down to the dungeon," he said, wiping his hands on his handkerchief as he stood. "I need them as bait for Commander Finn. Make sure word gets back to Queen Gisla's court that we have captured his favorite pets."

Aein's heart sank as the panic rose. They had walked into a trap. In trying to save their friend, they were about to become the very reason for his ruin.

"No!" said Aein, struggling.

"Don't be afraid to rough her up a bit if she doesn't play nice," said Lord Arnkell as he walked away. He stopped himself, though, and turned back. "Stick that other one in a silver harness. I'll be down to interrogate them immediately. Wouldn't want them to enjoy the relief of sunset."

Aein tried to carry herself with dignity, but her captors took Lord Arnkell's words to heart, dragging her when they decided she was not walking fast enough. They shoved her and then kicked her when she fell. She tasted the sharp, metallic flavor of blood.

"Better wipe yourself, missy," said one of the guards, a man she once trained with named Egill. "You'll drip on our nice clean floor."

She lifted the back of her hand to her lips. It was covered in red. "Why are you doing this?" she asked. "You know me."

"I don't know who you are or why, after Lord Arnkell

took you in and brought you up, you would poison every man, woman, and child in this fortress."

"That's not what happened—" she started to say.

But he cut her off. "I was there. I was there at the wedding. I lost my sister and my wife to those mushrooms you brought back. I saw it all."

And Aein realized she could say nothing to make this man see any different. Because the truth of the matter was that she had done it. She had poisoned everyone. It was not her fault. Lord Arnkell commanded it. Cook Bolstad told her to do it. But how to explain that to someone who had lost everything?

"When you're put on the rack, we'll all be lining up to give the wheel a turn," he hissed.

"Don't listen to him, Aein," said Lars, earning himself a clout to the side of his face. But he kept talking. "He doesn't know Lord Arnkell made you do it. He doesn't know it was all a plot to destroy the Kingdom of Haidra."

Egill lifted a thick boot and kicked Lars in the side of the knee, sending him to the ground in pain. "Shut up, Lars. I never would have taken you to turn against your own people. What did this pretty, little girl promise you? That she loved you? That she'd make you a happy man? "

"She knows of a cure," Lars said.

"Stop!" said Aein, terrified of what he was about to say.

"You can't kill her," Lars added. "You will never learn how to stop the shift without her."

"You people will say anything to keep yourself alive."

"Don't say another word," Aein hissed at her friend.

"Oh? Is this something special shared just between you two?" Egill lifted up Lars by the back of his shirt and pushed him forward. "Don't worry. Lord Arnkell loves hearing secrets and I'm sure you'll be dying to tell him before the night is through." The door to the dungeon opened and they were both thrown inside.

It was the same room where Aein had tried to sort out

the werewolves, where she had tried to isolate the wolves of night from the wolves of day so they would not kill one another. And now it was to be her prison.

The walls had once been whitewashed, but now were covered in unthinkable stains. The floor was stone. Two iron-barred jail cells sat next to each other. The bars had been painted with silver since Aein had last been here.

Roughly, Egill stripped off their armor, leaving them in nothing but the faded green uniforms of Lord Arnkell's dead soldiers and the silver harnesses should either of them choose to shift.

Egill threw them both into the same cell and turned the key. He peered through the bars with righteous glee. "Lord Arnkell has a talent for getting people chatty. He's quite the conversationalist. I'd recommend making it last as long as you can, because when he's satisfied he's learned everything in those pretty heads of yours? He's going to throw you in a pit with the wolves you created. He's going to start by feeding them one of your fingers and then maybe one of your toes. Whatever is lying around. And then he's going to let them rip you apart. But don't you worry, we'll make sure to pull them back if they're doing it too quick. We'll make sure you have plenty of time to savor the experience of being eaten alive, to get a full understanding of what you did. You're going to be begging for death. And when they're done with you? We'll take your heads and put them on spikes and let the birds peck your eyes from your skulls. And even all that, I would say, is letting you two off easy for the curse you brought into these walls. As you scream out for mercy, I want you to think of everyone who would be alive, who begged for mercy, who would still be with us if it wasn't for you."

And then he walked away.

Aein slumped to the floor, covering her mouth with her hands. She knew every word Egill said was true. This was the fate which awaited them. There would be no avoiding it. And the worst part was she did deserve it. Egill was right. She was responsible. No amount of apologizing or explaining she did not know what she was doing would change that fact. If it wasn't for her, none of this would have happened. She was responsible for the death of that man's sister and wife. She was responsible for all of the death around them.

Lars crouched beside her and took her hands in his, pulling them away from her face. "Aein?" he said. "Don't listen to a word he said. He is not telling the truth."

"But he is," Aein said, unable to keep her body from shaking violently.

"He is just trying to build the fear."

"It is working."

"Aein?" said Lars, sitting down and wrapping his arm around her shoulders. "When they bring you in to torture you, tell them whatever it is they want to hear. Don't try to be brave. Don't try to save anyone. They'll get it out of you one way or another, so say it at the beginning and save yourself."

Aein could not believe what Lars was saying. "If they find out... if they know what we know... if they get there and..." She scanned the barred window outside the cell block for any sign of life. She knew someone must be listening on the other side. She lowered her voice. "If Lord Arnkell finds out about what we found in the swamp and gets to it before Queen Gisla, everyone will be destroyed. No one will be able to stop the shift. Everything will crumble."

"It doesn't matter, Aein," said Lars. He took her face in his hands and smiled. "We're dead. You and me? We're gone from this world. If everyone on this planet becomes a werewolf, it doesn't matter. Our story is done. Let them fight it out among themselves. Let them kill each other off."

"You don't mean that," said Aein.

"Really?" said Lars, kissing her cheeks. "You think I

don't? Lord Arnkell left me in that swamp to die. He made you turn your best friends into werewolves because he wanted more land. I killed my friends. Our friends are about to kill us. Don't you see? Right? Good? It doesn't exist. Whoever has the power? He wins. And right now, that is Lord Arnkell. He's got all of these people believing he can save them from their problems and they are willing to do anything for him. They're so blinded by his pretty words, they're not even paying attention to what he's saying. They are going to sacrifice themselves to fix a problem he created. And Aein? It doesn't matter. Queen Gisla would do the exact same thing."

"No, she wouldn't..." Aein protested.

Lars laughed. There was a harsh edge to his chuckle. "You think she wouldn't? She sent her troops into the swamp where they were slaughtered by a harpy."

"That was not her fault. She was trying to hold the border and keep everyone safe—"

His voice thickened. "She sent in another group, who was also killed. And then what does she do? She sends in us. It would have just been you and me if Finn hadn't forced her to let him go. Three people. She sent three people to hold the border. And why? Because saving that precious cure is more important than our lives. She should have sent an army, Aein, but she didn't. Save yourself. She doesn't care about you. You are a pawn. Tell Lord Arnkell whatever he wants to hear."

"Stop this," said Aein.

"You need to stop following these leaders blindly just because they were anointed by someone at some time as a leader," explained Lars. "You were moon-eyed over Lord Arnkell—"

"Stop."

"You think the entire castle didn't notice the way you doted on him, the way you were ready to do anything to get him to notice you?"

"Why are you saying this?" she asked.

"And then the way you were able to just flip sides and join Queen Gisla. Why was that? Was it because Finn swept you off your feet?"

"No! I was trying to save our lives!"

"Our lives can't be saved anymore, Aein. You're in a cell, about to be tortured and then killed, all to protect the one person, our very own Queen Gisla, whose decisions put you here."

"I was trying to save you," she wept. Her face was hot and sweaty as she clung to his torso. His chest rose and fell, but caught on his breath.

"I am already lost," he replied, wiping away her tears. His voice cracked. "You are already lost. All that remains is how badly it is going to hurt before we die."

The door opened and a hooded man walked into the room flanked by two guards. "Lord Arnkell requests the pleasure of your company."

CHAPTER FIFTEEN

The room was dark and sweltering. There were no windows, no way for anyone to know who was inside and what was being done to them.

On the far wall was a fireplace. Metal pokers heated in the coals beside the bellows, ready for use whenever the mood struck. Manacles hung from the ceiling. On a bench were wicked looking instruments - knives and pincers and spoons with sharp edges.

In the center was a flat table. They dragged Lars in and forced him down. He struggled as they bound his wrists and ankles in silver cuffs. The cuffs were attached to two giant wheels at either end, which could be turned to stretch him until his limbs ripped out of their sockets.

They threw Aein into a chair and bolted her hands and legs into place with silver straps. It faced the rack so that she would have to see everything they did to Lars. Lord Arnkell walked into the room, taking off his gloves and smiling at the sight as if it were a pleasant picnic on a sunny day.

"We have until sunset until they change. Let's make sure we make the most of it, shall we?" he said to the torturer. He came over and crouched before Aein.

"Knowing you're a woman of reason, I thought we might start by asking you a few questions. Now, I should warn you, you will want to think hard before you open your mouth. If you tell the truth, everyone will be safe and sound. But if you answer and I think you are lying to me, we're going to give that wheel a turn."

Lars fixed his eyes on the ceiling as they turned the rack, pulling his body taut. He clenched his teeth and grunted, but he did not look at Aein. Her throat became dry, realizing that if she told Lord Arnkell everything, the Haidra kingdom would fall. Everyone would be trapped as a werewolf forever. Civil war would kill thousands of people as they rebelled against Queen Gisla. But if she didn't speak, she would have to watch the man she loved being torn apart. Her decision alone would determine how much pain he endured before he died.

"Shall we begin?" asked Lord Arnkell. He picked up one of the daggers and tested the tip of it on his thumb. "First question, why did you poison my people and bring about this war?"

Aein fumbled, unsure how to answer. "You made me," she answered truthfully.

Lord Arnkell waved his hand and the wheel on the rack turned another notch.

"NO!" cried Aein. She looked up at Lord Arnkell. "What do you expect me to say?" she asked. "You know and I know the truth. I am telling you the truth!"

Lord Arnkell held the blade inches from her cheek. His eyes were dark and soulless. It was like staring into the eyes of a reptile. "I want you to admit you are responsible for everything that happened here."

"I am," she said. "I am completely and totally responsible for everything that happened."

"AEIN!" cried out Lars, trying to get her to stop.

Lord Arnkell turned to the scribe. "Be sure to note the prisoner confessed to treason."

Aein watched in horror as the man wrote down the

words onto a parchment. She had signed her own death warrant; she had given Lord Arnkell exactly what he needed to feed her to the werewolves. But it was the truth.

"Now, would you like to tell me why you committed this act?" asked Lord Arnkell. There was a warning on his face, some message that Aein could not read. What could he possibly want her to say?

"Cook Bolstad told me to," she replied, terrified it was the wrong answer.

Lord Arnkell tutted, but he did not motion for another turn of the wheel. "How fortunate you are able to blame a dead man for your treason. To place the blame at the feet of someone who is not here to defend himself." Lord Arnkell walked around in a circle. "What did that old fool give you that keeps you from turning?"

"He... he didn't give me anything..." said Aein.

Lord Arnkell motioned to the rack and Lars let out a terrible, high pitched scream as his bones were pulled from their sockets.

"I swear!" said Aein.

"You told us it was a white mushroom with brown flecks," said Lord Arknell. "Where did you find them?"

Aein remembered back to the night that Lord Arnkell captured her and tied her to a tree for the wild werewolves to tear apart. She had told him a lie. She had told him there was another mushroom. She tried to remember her lie.

She didn't answer fast enough and the torturer turned the rack another click.

"One of our men stopped shifting into madness the morning after we captured you. He said he ate something from your pack but did not see what it was."

Sweat prickled on Aein's forehead. She remembered. There had been one berry she had missed and he had eaten it.

Lord Arnkell leaned into Aein. "He said it didn't taste

like a mushroom. He said it tasted like a fruit. You wouldn't have been lying to me about the white mushrooms now, would you?" he asked.

She looked at Lars. He was panting from exertion, trying not to cry out. His wavy, auburn hair dripped with sweat. Blood trickled from his feet and hands where the manacles cut into his skin. But he would not look at Aein. He was letting her make the choice - him or an entire kingdom filled with people who loved and laughed.

"Oh, he can't help you," said Lord Arnkell, pointing at Lars. But then he paused, taking in the unspoken energy between his two prisoners. "Perhaps we have been going about this wrong. You seem a little distracted, Aein. I need to make sure that you are giving me your full and undivided attention." He turned to the torturer and said, "Get a hot poker and take out her eye."

"I know where it is!" shouted Lars. The torture stopped. "She had never been to the swamp before and I led her to the clearing with the white mushrooms!" he cried. "She can't tell you because she doesn't know where they are. I'm the one who knows the swamp."

Lord Arnkell snapped around to face Lars. A slow, satisfied smile crept across his face. "My. Of all my soldiers, I am surprised you're the one to speak. She must be very important to you, Lars."

"Just don't hurt her and I'll take you to them," he panted. "I'll show you. They are in the swamp. It was a mushroom she ate, a mushroom she said tasted like a berry."

Aein realized Lars needed help to lend credibility to his lie. She shouted, "Stop, Lars! Don't tell him!"

It earned her a cuff to the side of her head that left her ears ringing, but the bluff seemed to have worked.

"White mushrooms that taste like a berry?" asked Lord Arnkell, leaning forward with interest. "Are you sure it wasn't a berry?"

Lars nodded his head. "We went back to the swamp to

collect more. They are in season. We were about to harvest them all when your men happened upon us."

"How fortunate you eluded them," Lord Arnkell hissed.

"If you eat enough of this mushroom," said Lars, "you can stop the shift. Aein ate it the morning we first arrived. I ate the brown mushrooms and now shift. Aein ate the white mushrooms and she is immune."

Lord Arnkell's mouth opened slightly. "Fully immune?" he said.

Aein spat at his feet, earning herself another blow. But her perceived reluctance to talk made them believe the story.

"And why have you not eaten this white mushroom?" asked Lord Arnkell.

Lars was focused upon Aein as if somehow he could communicate his plan to her through the power of his thoughts. "There wasn't enough. We were supposed to bring it back to Queen Gisla."

"What a good little soldier," said Lord Arnkell. He motioned to the torturer to reduce the pressure. He turned back to Aein. "Don't worry. As soon as he shifts, all of these nuisances will go away and he'll be right as rain in the morning. You, on the other hand, I believe do not shift," he said, taking a threatening step towards her.

"I'll take you to the harvest," Lars promised, his voice desperate. "They are growing now. When Queen Gisla hears you've captured us, she won't come. We mean nothing to her. We're foot soldiers. We're the price of war. She'll go straight to the mushrooms, I promise you. You may kill us, but Queen Gisla will still have won."

Lord Arnkell tapped the knife on his front teeth. "Hmmm…"

"I vow I will take you to them if you promise not to touch her."

Lord Arnkell turned back to Aein and smiled pleasantly. "I promise not to touch her unless you make me. If you lead me to this mushroom and it ends the shift of my good and honest people, I will give you both a day's head start before I set my hunters on you." Lord Arnkell turned to his guards. "Take Finn and get him cleaned up. We leave before sunset."

As they were releasing his bonds, he begged, "What of Aein?"

Lord Arnkell seemed mystified by Lars's question. "I am not touching her. It is so easy to lose people. I think it might be safest to leave her here in this exact spot until we get back."

"You can't leave her chained to that chair for the months it will take for us to get to the swamp and back again," said Lars.

"Yes, I can," stated Lord Arnkell flatly. "You made me promise not to touch her, and so I shall not. So you had better be quick and not dilly-dally on the road. Every day you delay is a day she is trapped down here. I think it will prove very educational for her to witness any interrogations that need to take place while I am gone, to see the fate that she sidestepped because you were loyal enough to tell your lord and master the truth. Who knows? Perhaps she will grow so attached to this place, she'll never leave again." He turned to the guard. "If for some reason you think she is trying to escape, break her legs."

"That was not a part of the deal!" shouted Lars as the lifted him off the rack. "I won't show you anything if you hurt her!"

His body was limp and he was unable to hold himself up. Two soldiers had to carry him as his legs dragged behind. His green eyes, full of tears, looked back at Aein and she realized this was the last time she would ever see him. They would kill him as soon as they got to the swamp and realized he had lied. But he had bought them both time.

"Like I said, I won't harm either of you unless you

make me." Lord Arnkell leaned forward into Aein's face. "Don't give us a reason to hurt you and everything will be fine."

She watched as Lars was dragged away. She did not struggle. She did not make any sign that she was anything but broken and defeated. It seemed to please the torturer, for he left the room with a whistle.

"I'll be back to see how you are doing in a few days," he said. "Say hello to my rat friends, won't you?"

Aein looked over. In the corner, a whiskered nose was sniffing the air. They must have known to come out for the bits of meat and blood left in the room after an interrogation. They had been robbed of a meal this time. Aein wondered how long it would be before they decided she was just as tasty.

CHAPTER SIXTEEN

Aein heard the party leaving. The cheers from the people, the sound of hooves and horses echoed down the empty stone halls. And from that point on, she lost count of the days. The rats came. Hungry, they bit her. Her ankles and wrists bolted in place, she could do nothing more than wiggle her legs to try and fling them aside. Every so often, the jailor came to lift a mouthful of water to her lips. At some point, some stale, moldy bread was forced into her mouth. It was the most delicious thing she ever tasted. They gave her just enough food to keep her alive, but not enough to give her strength. Her body was covered in sores from being unable to move. It seemed like every time she fell asleep, someone would run a metal rod across the bars of the door or the rats would test to see if she was still alive. She began to pray for death. She would drift off, and in her mind, she would be back at the campsite there in the swamp with Finn staring into the sky and Cook Bolstad telling her to find him.

She was dreaming again of the same place, but this time, for the first time, Finn turned to her and whispered, "Aein?"

She smiled. It was so good to hear his voice.

"Aein?"

And then she realized she was not dreaming. That the voice was real. She pried open her crusty eyes and tried to lift her head. Everything was blurry. There was a single candle. Holding it was a man who seemed like Finn.

"Finn...?" she croaked. Her voice sounded strange in her throat. Perhaps he was an apparition. Perhaps he was nothing more than the guard come down to break her legs because she screamed in her sleep.

"Dammnit," said the man who looked like Finn.

He set down the candle and suddenly, his large, calloused hands were on either side of her cheeks, lifting up her face so that she didn't have to expend the energy. It was him. His blue eyes were crinkled with worry and she wanted to tell him it was okay. She hadn't tried to escape. They hadn't broken her legs. She stayed right where she was supposed to, just like she promised.

With one hand, Finn cradled her neck, and with the other, took a canteen from his side and poured a few drops into her mouth. He wiped away the bit that ran out the side with his thick thumb.

She leaned forward to gulp down more, but he pulled it away. "Slow down," he said, putting it on the floor for a moment. "You figure out if what I gave you is going to stay where it is should in your belly and then I'll give you more."

He fiddled with her restraints. With just a touch, he was able to free the pins that held her manacles in place - four simple pieces of metal which held her captive. She tried to stand, but failed and slumped into him.

"Careful! Careful," he said, wrapping his arm around her waist.

He smelled of leather and his horse and Aein smiled. He felt as strong as a tree.

"We need to get you out of here, but I'm going to need your help." He lifted up the flask of water and gave her another mouthful, as tenderly as a parent feeding a sick child.

She coughed as it went down wrong and he paused. "How did you find me?" she whispered.

"You wouldn't believe me if I told you," he said, putting his canteen away and scanning the room.

"Try me."

"I had a dream."

She gave him a sleepy smile and ran her finger along his silvery scar. "Me, too…"

He hoisted her upright as she began to sink into unconsciousness. "Stay with me!"

"I am so tired…"

"We'll sleep on the way," he said.

"I wish I was a bird…" she murmured as the darkness called her so sweetly.

"What?" he asked.

"I wish I could shift into one of those birds that were spying on us and then wake up in the morning whole and happy just like you wolves." She was so tired. She couldn't help the fat, exhausted tear which rolled down her cheek. "But I can't. I can't just go to sleep and wake up like the world has never changed."

"You're rambling. Getting you out of this dungeon will change you enough," Finn promised, urging her to keep fighting. "Come on, Aein. I need your help."

She fought the desire to surrender. "We have to get Cook Bolstad's cookbook," she said.

"What?" said Finn. "There is no time."

She shook her head and it made her dizzy. "Take me to the passage," she begged. "Get me out and leave me there, but you have to get the cookbook. Cook Bolstad told me to find him. It was in the dream. All we have of him is that cookbook."

Finn seemed so torn by her request. "I can't believe I am going to do this," he said. He threw her over his shoulder upside-down and carried her out of the room.

One hand held his sword, the other gripped her legs.

Her mind began to clear and she began to realize what was going on. The hallway was dark and quiet. Moonlight shone in through the windows, but the torches had all been extinguished. They passed the prison guard. His body leaned against the wall covered in crimson. His throat had been slit. There were legs beneath tables and slumped forms behind tapestries. She realized Finn had come in as an assassin. He left no one in his path alive. He was prepared to kill without mercy everyone in the Arnkell stronghold to save her. He had done all of this for her.

They reached the hidden passageway and he lowered her to the floor behind the tapestry. He took her face in his hands and brushed back her filthy, greasy hair. He gave her a little more water and this time, soaked some bread in it and placed it in the palm of her hand. "Stay right here. Stay as quiet as a fawn in the tall grass. I will be back." He stared at her as if he almost couldn't leave her, as if he was terrified she would disappear if he went. But he did. He kissed her forehead and then was gone.

Slowly, bite by painful bite, Aein ate the bread. She wanted to tear into it, to devour it like a starving animal, but it was as if her mouth had forgotten how to chew, her throat forgotten how to swallow. But when the food finally went down, it hit her system like wine. She wanted to laugh it felt so good. She was going to live. She rested her head against the wall. She was going to live...

Finn seemed like he had been gone forever. The entire stronghold was silent. Not a single patrol marched by. Not a servant or a reveler. She strained her ears for some sound. It was taking too long. Her heart began pounding as she wondered if she had sent Finn to his death. She imagined him slaughtered. She imagined him bleeding just feet away from her. She imagined him captured and on the rack where Lars had been, refusing to tell them she was hidden behind a piece of fabric in the hallway.

She startled as the corner of the tapestry pushed back. She had not heard any feet approach, no sound or stir in the air. It was Finn. He was alive and in his arms he carried Cook Bolstad's book.

"Is this it?" he asked, kneeling down beside her.

Aein sobbed and nodded, throwing her arms around his neck and squeezing him so tight he could barely breathe.

"Hey, now... shhh..." he murmured, stroking her back. "I'm here. I have you." He kept repeating it over and over again until she believed him. He kept saying it and rocking her until she loosened her grip. He gently handed the book to her. "Can you carry this? Can I give you this and the light?"

Having a job made it easier to focus. Clutching the book to her chest, she struggled to her knees, wobbling like a newborn colt.

"We need to get going," he said, pushing the door open behind her and handing her the lantern. "Are you ready?"

"Yes," she said. She peered into the darkness of the cavern and a chill ran up her spine. "Do you think there are guards in there?"

"There were a few," Finn replied. He did not have to say any more. Aein understood what happened.

He leaned Aein against one arm and tucked his other beneath her knees, scooping her up like she weighed no more than a kitten. Aein rested the lantern on her stomach, allowing the warmth to seep into her bones and chase away the chill. She leaned her head against his chest and could feel his heart beating like a butterfly against her cheek.

They made their way through the cavern in silence. As the light illuminated their path, there were shapes and bodies kicked to the side. Pools of blood stained the already dark ground.

Finally, they emerged. There was a single horse waiting.

Aein and Lars's mounts were long since gone, along with all of their goods and supplies. Finn placed her atop the horse and climbed up behind her. He wrapped one arm tightly around her waist and with the other, took the reins and urged the horse forward. In the distance, a bell began to toll.

"We've been found out." He clicked his tongue and urged the horse into a gallop, streaming along the road to put as must distance between them and the castle as possible. Aein clung to consciousness as best she could, knowing only the movement of the horse beneath her and the strength of Finn holding her up. How long they rode, she did not know. The heaving breath and pounding hooves of the horse was the only sound that punctuated the night. After what seemed like hours, Finn slowed the horse to a walk and then to a stop beside a river.

"The sun will be rising soon. We need to rest," he whispered in Aein's ear, his rough stubble tickling her cheek.

She managed to nod and keep her seat as he dismounted. He reached up and caught her as she ungracefully fell from the saddle. Her body ached from riding, the muscles required to keep her seat not having been used since the day she had been captured.

But Finn would not allow her to collapse onto the ground. Instead, he placed his arm around her and leaned her body against his. "Let's see if you can remember how to walk," he said.

Slowly she stumbled beside him. He stopped frequently to give her more water and more food. To keep her mind off the agony of retraining her muscles, he tried to keep a conversation flowing.

"So abandoned your post in the swamp?" he tried to joke. "I know the fog is miserable, but this seems a little extreme."

"We were trying to save you," Aein grunted, trying to make her rubbery legs put one foot in front of the other.

"Seems like things didn't go according to plan."

"Well, first off, you weren't there."

"I could have told you that."

"Next time, I'll remember to ask," Aein winced.

Finn laughed. Laughter seemed like such a strange sound in Aein's ears. He pressed a kiss into the top of her head and buried his lips into her hair. "What could possibly make you think I was down in Lord Arnkell's dungeon? Where was your head that you thought you could take on an entire stronghold to get me out?"

"You just made the same choice," she reminded him, jerking her thumb back to where they had just ridden. The movement was enough to throw her off-balance.

"I'm different," he said, heaving her slipping body up higher with a grunt. "I do this all the time."

"Well, I decided to go for some advanced training," she retorted. "It was either take on an entire stronghold or go back and tell Queen Gisla we misplaced you. I decided I'd take my chances with the Arnkell torture chamber."

"It helps if you don't get captured."

"I shall make note." Aein groaned. "Can't we stop? Just for a moment?"

Finn lowered her to the ground. The moon was low on the horizon and the sky was beginning to show the signs of false dawn. Her legs no longer felt like rubber. They were on fire with pins and needles. She pounded on them with her fist, trying to make it go away.

"Really? Why were you there?" he asked again, sitting down beside her. This time, she could tell he wanted the truth.

"Some of Lord Arnkell's men came to the swamp," Aein explained. "They told us you had been caught."

"Did you escape them or did they bring you here?" he asked, pressing for more information, as if he needed to know if there were more people who needed to pay for Aein's suffering.

She closed her eyes, remembering the claws of the

harpy digging into her shoulder, the feel of her knife driving into the creature's skin. "We were attacked by a harpy. She killed everyone. I had on a silver harness and it protected me."

"Who made the kill?"

"I did," said Aein. The fight was so long ago and the victory seemed so hollow.

He ripped a piece of grass from the ground, unable to look up at her. "And Lars? Did the harpy..."

His voice trailed off and Aein realized he assumed Lars was dead. She grabbed his arm. "He's alive," she reassured him.

Finn stiffened. "Did I leave him behind?" He was almost on his feet, ready to race back before she could stop him.

"No!" said Aein. "No. He's with Lord Arnkell." A shadow passed over Finn's face and she could see him jump to the conclusion that Lars had defected. "No. He did it to save me. They were going to gouge out my eyes and he couldn't take it. He's leading them to the swamp."

"He told them of the bush?" clarified Finn. His face became hard and serious.

Aein shook her head. "He told them that a mushroom is the cure. He said that he would only show it to them if I was kept alive and unharmed." Aein felt a lump rise in her throat and a tightness in her chest. She blinked away the tears. "They'll kill him once they find out he lied."

At that moment, the birds began to wake up and the morning was filled with song. A breeze blew through the trees as Finn inched his body closer to her and took her hands in his. "We'll get him back," he promised.

"How?" she asked, the hopelessness of it all too much to bear. "He is probably already dead."

Finn set his jaw. "Have I ever lied to you, Aein?"

"No," she replied.

"Then trust me. We will get him back."

She gazed in to his beautiful eyes, the eyes of this man

who fought an entire castle to bring her to safety. She raised her fingertips and touched the scar which ran across his face from that time he had saved her before. It was one of the things she loved most about his face.

He lifted his mouth to hers. He smelled of leather and himself. His lips touched hers lightly, and then with more insistence as she kissed him back. A warmth spread through her tired body, pushing aside the pain and aches and filling her with want and need.

And yet, despite wanting him, despite wanting to be here with him in this moment, she found herself placing her hands upon his strong, broad chest and pushing him away. "I can't... Lars and I..."

She did not have to say more. She could see it took every ounce of control he had, but he rolled onto his back and covered his eyes with the back of his hand. He nodded in understanding. "Of course," he said. "You and Lars."

She reached out and took his hand, interlacing her fingers in his, realizing that she did not want to say no to this man. She did not want to stop this person who had moved heaven and earth to save her. "I made a promise..."

He smiled, but there was pain and heartbreak in that smile. "Then you must keep it," he said.

They lay there together silently, hands entwined and gazing at the sky until the stars faded and the sun came up, both thinking about how sometimes the world could go so terribly wrong.

CHAPTER SEVENTEEN

When the shift came, Finn looked at Aein one last time before his hand disappeared and his face disappeared and all that was left was his eyes gazing into her soul, wanting her but knowing there was nothing she could give.

She turned onto her side and pushed herself to her hands and knees. Their brief rest was not enough, but who knew how quickly the Arnkell stronghold would mobilize and send people after them. Who knew if the time they wasted on a nap might cost Lars his life.

She tried to stand, but her legs buckled and collapsed under her. She punched the ground in frustration.

She felt a furry head work its way between her arms. She looked down, confused by what was happening. Finn wiggled until he was beneath her and then he stood, lifting her body with his. She leaned against his powerful shoulders, letting him support her upper body as her legs tried to follow. He walked her over to the horse, who was still saddled from their earlier ride. She rested her hand upon the stirrup and wondered how she would ever be able to climb up. She could see Finn realize this was something they should have addressed before the shift.

But the sight of his worry, of him taking the

responsibility for this moment of difficulty, fueled her with strength. She hauled herself into a standing position, clinging to the saddle and praying the horse would not walk away. It seemed like the animal understood she was in dire need of gentle understanding. He stood patiently as she tried to figure out what to do next.

It was Finn, again, who came up with a plan. He nosed her foot. Mystified, she lifted it and he stepped beneath her, volunteering his back as a step. She straightened her leg and he stood, bringing her high enough that she was able to scramble over. She clung to the horse's neck, terrified she might not have the strength to hold on. She managed not to fall off that day.

As the miles and hours and days went by, Aein began to recover her strength. The access to food and water did more for her than almost everything else. She and Finn talked no more of what had passed between them. He insisted they travel by day when he could run alongside in wolf form, saying it would be easier on the horse to have only one rider, though they walked the horse together after the sun went down.

Finn was nothing but gentle and helpful. Their conversation was polite, but distant, and disintegrated into small talk and idle chat. He hid behind his mask of respect and duty, and the mystery of what could have been between them, what was once between them, made Aein's heart break a little.

But the drive to save Lars pushed them on and kept Aein from trying to heal the rift. If he was alive, this detachment would be for the best. And if he was dead, there would be other things to worry about.

They reached the marsh surrounding the swamp in less than a week and a half, faster than Aein had ever made the journey on her own. The wooden pier through the bog waited for them, but the sun was still high in the sky.

Aein dismounted and bent to stretch her legs. Finn waited for her patiently. She shielded her eyes with her hand. "Finn?" she said. "I don't want to make this rescue with you as a wolf." The thought of entering the forest and facing the fog on her own was terrifying. The thought of fighting a monster when she could barely run was even worse. "If Lars is alive, he'll be human now and there is no telling how badly they've hurt him. If we wait to rescue him after the shift, he'll have healed. He'll be stronger."

Finn regarded her for a few minutes more and then sneezed. She hoped that was his way of saying he would go along with her plan.

"It will also be dark," she continued, "and it will be easier for us to hide. This is the only road in or out. They probably have it well guarded."

Finn sneezed, but this time twice.

"Plus, it will be good if we're well rested before we go into a battle..." she finished lamely. Despite all of the good reasons to delay, she wondered if waiting to rush into swamp would mean they missed a crucial moment to save Lars. She could not tell if Finn agreed with her wholeheartedly or not, but he did not block her way as she led the horse into the brush and unrolled the bed. She took off the saddle and left the horse to graze freely. Finn sat on his haunches and watched unblinking. She crawled into the blanket and rested her head in her arm.

"So... you have first watch?" she asked him. She pointed towards the road. "You're supposed to look out there for danger, not stare at me."

But he did not move. She wondered what was going on. She closed her eyes, willing herself to get what sleep she could before twilight, when she felt soft footsteps tentatively creep beside her. She was so scared of frightening him off she didn't even breathe. She just waited, pretending to rest. And then slowly, gently, Finn lowered himself beside her, pressing his body against her belly so that she was spooning him tight. She inched her arm across him, burying her face in his dark fur. He released a heavy sigh. She realized this would be the last time they ever had this moment. No matter how things unfolded in the next few hours, their lives would change forever.

She woke as the sun set, feeling Finn's shift. Gently, he rose from the bed, trying not to disturb her, and she fought the urge to call him back. Aein could not help a twinge of sadness. She uncurled and sat up, acting as if she hadn't been awake all along. "Is it time?" she asked.

Finn stared at her in silence for what seemed to be an eternity. The thoughts running across his face were unfathomable. But he just nodded and said, "Yes."

Aein rose and went to put the bedroll away. Finn stopped her. "Leave it all here," he directed. "We need stealth, not speed. We'll go as far as we can on the road, past the bog, and then wade into the swamp through the trees."

Aein fought a shiver, thinking of the creatures who lurked off the path. "That's a death sentence."

"For those who have not been in the swamp," said Finn as he removed his armor and hid it beneath some brush. "But not you. You know how to survive."

He said it as a statement of fact. There was no hint that it was false praise to buoy Aein's spirit. It rang with as much truth as if he had said she had two arms and two legs. And Aein realized he was right. She did know how to survive. She faced the fog and had not gone mad. She fought a cyclops and a harpy and werewolves and survived. She had lived when everyone else around her died.

"Those soldiers riding with Lord Arnkell," continued Finn, stripping off his chainmail, "some of them may have been to the border before, but my bet is that most of them have not. If they had, they would have understood why holding the line was so important."

Aein nodded, beginning to see his plan. "They'll think we're creatures of the fog."

"They have no idea you escaped," Finn pointed out. "No reason to think you should be here. They'll think you're a ghost." He gave her a wink. "What do you say we give them a good haunting?"

The smile slowly crept across Aein's face. "I hope we frighten them to death."

CHAPTER EIGHTEEN

Aein held Cook Bolstad's book and ran her hand across its cover. She opened it, and the paper released the smells of the kitchen, the smell of him. Fry oils and old onions and hearth smoke, scents that couldn't wash off in a basin. Cook Bolstad had flipped through each loved page. She could even see places where his fingers left a smudge or a stain. She had no idea what the book said, but it was too precious to lose. It was the only thing she had of his, this man who raised her. She wrapped it in one of Finn's less stained shirts, and tucked it into the crook of a tree for safe keeping. As soon as she found someone who could read, she would make that person go through it with her page-by-page and explain every wavy, black line and picture.

Aein tucked her blonde hair into the back of her shirt and went off to find Finn. There was a half-moon on the rise and it lit the land just enough to see. Finn was kneeling on the planked road, smearing mud from the bog all over himself. There were enough frogs singing that Aein knew they could speak in hushed tones without being overheard, but Finn said nothing when she sat next to him. He just lifted a handful of the sludge and wiped it over her hair and skin. Wordlessly, he slid a silver dagger over to her, keeping the sword for himself.

And then he pushed himself up from the road with his knuckles and ran.

On tiptoe, he tore off down the pier, keeping his body in a half-crouch. Aein chased after him, her lungs burning. She dare not breathe heavily. She prayed she would not trip on the planks. She just kept her eyes on Finn and tried to keep up.

He held up his fist and slowed to a creep.

The swamp was directly ahead of them. The branches of the sunken trees looked like claws. The bog had given way to the algae covered water.

But coming out of the swamp was the sound of clashing metal and terrified cries. Aein gulped, wondering what had attacked and who was on the defensive. But Finn did not stop. Instead, he watched the entrance to the swamp intently as he lowered himself off the side of the road. He did not look back to see if Aein followed. Either she was there or she was not. Aein quietly sat and put her feet in. The water was warm and it felt like bathing in old stew. She tried not to flinch as something brushed past her leg, telling herself it was just a branch, knowing full well that it was not. The water came up to her chest before her feet touched the bottom.

They waded forward, trying to move without disturbing the surface. Aein silently scooped away the algae as it piled against her. As they approached the finger-like roots of the mangroves, the noise of the battle became louder and it continued to grow the deeper they went into the swamp.

Aein was grateful that Finn kept the wooden path within sight of the road, but even more grateful that they had not taken it. Through the branches, Aein saw five soldiers illuminated by torchlight. They were waving the fire at a monster with six legs who stood at least ten-feet tall. Aein froze in fear. His torso was that of a man, his body that of a scorpion. His name was something told late at night around the hearth to scare small children - a girtablilu. Aein remembered the folk stories. This creature was said to open the doors to the land of darkness. Aein tried to remember how he could be defeated when, with his great pincer claw, the girtablilu cut one of the men in half.

Finn wrapped his hand over her mouth, smothering the scream in her throat. The urge to attack the monster blinded her, tearing through her mind as the most important thing to do. But Finn held her there in silence. He whispered in her ear, "They are distracted. This is what we need to free Lars."

She breathed, forcing herself to think through the primitive battle-lust. It would get her killed. She needed to hold on to it and use it for Lars. She nodded her head in agreement and he slowly removed his hand.

Quietly, they continued on, following the planked road but staying in the dark shadows. Firelight flickered in front of them once again and Aein was horrified to see where it was coming from.

"They are in the clearing," she hissed. "How could Lars have led them to the clearing?"

Through the trees, she could see Lars staked in the center of the camp like a guard dog outside a shop. He wore the silver harness and his skin wept from bloody welts beneath it. His great head rested between his paws; his eyes were faded and glassy.

"Lars!" breathed Aein, hoping no one else would hear them. But in the heat of the battle going on, she thought they were safe.

His ears pricked up, as if unable to believe they had heard the sound they just heard.

"LARS!" she whispered louder.

He stood up, staring at them intently.

"Don't give us away, you fool!" hissed Finn.

Lars immediately lay down again. The only sign that

something was going on was the tenseness in his body and the way his wolfish eyebrows flickered this way and that.

Aein and Finn crawled out of the water and into the clearing. Aein wanted to cry. The place was ruined. The grass was trampled to mud. Waste was thrown around the edges. The peace that had inhabited it seemed chased away. She cast her eyes towards the bush, unsure if the branches were withered or if it was just that it was still out of season. Surely after all this time there should have been a leaf or a bit of new growth.

Lars could not help his head popping up the moment he saw them. His body vibrated with excitement. Finn rushed over to free him from the silver harness while Aein ran over to the bush to see if it had been damaged. What if their decision to save Finn had led to the destruction of the only cure? What if Lars's feelings for her and his fear for her safety, what if his willingness to do anything to keep her safe, cost everyone their future?

Finn cursed. "Why won't this harness let me unbuckle you?"

Suddenly, a panting man raced into the clearing. Aein spun around, knife drawn and ready to throw.

Standing there, naked sword in hand, was Lord Arnkell. His eyes were wild and his face was white as a sheet. He stared at Aein in disbelief.

"Are you a trick of the fog?" he asked.

CHAPTER NINETEEN

"SPEAK!" he shouted at her. "Tell me if you are real or a phantom of the fog or I shall cut down this wolf that you once held so dear!"

Finn rose and pulled out his sword. Aein held up her hands to stop him. "I am real!" she said. "I am real..."

Lord Arnkell lowered his blade. He wiped his face with his hand. "Thank the gods. Oh thank the gods our prayers have been answered!"

But Finn was not ready to believe they were the answer to anyone's prayer, much less Lord Arnkell. He spun the hilt of his sword to adjust his grip, keeping the tip up and ready to fight. "Just let us go with our friend and we shall leave you forever..." warned Finn.

"No!" said Lord Arnkell, panicking. "NO! You cannot leave! You cannot leave us to these... these... things!"

Finn glanced back at Aein in confusion.

"What things?" asked Aein slowly.

"There are monsters," said Lord Arnkell, waving his sword out at the swamps. "There are monsters everywhere. We retreated here. It is the only place they cannot enter. We keep trying to leave the swamp, but the fog... the fog won't let us. It keeps turning our feet and we keep ending up here. Why won't it let us leave?"

Lars whimpered and she realized that while Lord Arnkell may not have set a trap for them, they were trapped nonetheless.

"What do you mean?" asked Finn.

Lord Arnkell seemed terrified and weak. Dark circles ringed his eyes and his face looked haggard and old. Aein realized it was the first time in his life he had not been in control. This was the first time he wasn't surrounded by people who were ready to make his nightmares go away. He had never been to the swamp before, never faced the fog, never seen the creatures of the border. He always sent someone else to do it. And for whatever reason, the swamp decided to give him a full taste of what he missed. He motioned impotently with his sword. "You have got to get us out of here."

"Why should we help you?" asked Aein.

"Because there are monsters here," explained Lord Arnkell, his eyes wild, "just like my father once warned me. They are coming through the border and soon the swamp will overtake the land. The edges are already shifting. It will eat up everything my family has fought for, just as the prophesies foretold. We have to stop these creatures before they get out. None of us will survive if we don't stop them." He threw aside his sword and fell against Finn, grabbing him by the shirt and begging on his knees. "We have been fighting the creatures of the swamp since the day we arrived. Since the moment we arrived! You must save me. I shall go mad!"

"You mean like you left Lars here in the swamp to go mad?" Aein reminded him.

"I was wrong..." blubbered Lord Arnkell. "I was a fool and didn't know..."

"I should run you through where you stand," said Finn, his words cold and impartial.

"You need me as much as I need you," warned Lord

Arnkell. "Just try to get back to the edge of the swamp. Just try. You'll see. You'll be picked off by harpies. Eaten by ogres. Set on fire by chimera. The swamp will never let you leave. There is only strength in numbers. Help me get out and I will help you get out, I promise."

"We will part ways the moment we reach the edge of the swamp?" said Aein.

"I promise," said Lord Arnkell, bobbing his head. "I promise you whatever you want. What do you want? Gold? Land? It is yours. Name your price."

Anything, Aein thought. She had gone from orphaned kitchen wench to reviled pariah to having her lord and master beg at her feet. She could ask him for anything in the world and he would make it hers. She looked at Lars and Finn. There was only one thing she wanted. "You shall call an immediate peace with the Haidra Kingdom and cease this war," said Aein.

"It is yours," he promised, desperately. "I swear it! It shall be the first thing I do."

Aein walked to Lars and placed her hand on his harness.

"Don't!" shouted Lord Arnkell. "He will attack you! They have all turned and attacked!"

Aein put her hand upon the buckles, her eyes never leaving the face of Lord Arnkell, just challenging him to stop her. He did not move a muscle. Aein released the harness and it fell to the ground with a clank. Lars got up, shaking his fur. And then he began to growl and advance upon Lord Arnkell.

Lord Arnkell fell back, tripping over himself and falling to the ground. "I told you! He is wild! He will kill us all! Strike him down!"

There was something about Lord Arnkell's fear, about his powerlessness, which delighted Aein. She should not have felt such joy to see him so weak, but she loved it. She loved watching him grovel and squirm and cry like a frightened child. There was a voice inside of her which seemed to whisper that she should command Lars to attack, she should let Lord Arnkell feel the pain he had inflicted on others and experience the fate he had doomed his people to.

And then she felt a hand upon her shoulder.

"Look down, Aein," Finn said calmly.

She glanced at her feet. The fog had breached the clearing. It wrapped itself around her ankles like shackles, chaining her to her hatred, and dooming Lars to memories of murder.

"Come back, Lars," she commanded.

The werewolf bared his teeth at Aein and snarled.

"Remember who I am," she said. "The fog is making you forget."

Lars continued to growl, but it was softer. It lacked the violence of his earlier threat. The removal of the silver and the pain which remained was tapping into his wildest survival instincts. But he was listening.

"Lars," said Aein. "The fog will try and trap us in the swamp. It is hiding the path. It wants us to destroy one another. It wants to keep us here for itself. Resist it, Lars."

A noise came from behind Lord Arnkell, a roar and the sound of battle cries.

"It's coming closer," he whispered, shaking in fear. "We need to go now."

"This way," said Finn, stepping into the water.

Lord Arnkell grabbed Finn's dripping sleeve. "NO! There are creatures in there ..."

"The road is blocked by a girtablilu," said Finn, shaking him off and pointing out what seemed like the obvious. "We shall die if we go that way. This is the only way out." He waded in deeper and Aein moved to join him. The sooner they left the swamp the better.

"Stop!" Lord Arnkell cried. "Do you think we have not tried? Do you think we have not attempted to get out that way? The moment you set foot in the water and head in any direction other than deeper into the swamp, the monsters will come for you. The fog will let you in, but it will not let you out. I left with one-hundred men, half of them werewolves. They are dead. Every one. That thing which looks like a scorpion is finishing off the last of them now. Not even my wolves survived. They found a way to snap their silver harnesses and killed one another."

"The wolves can't be killed except by silver or dismemberment," said Aein.

"Can't?" Lord Arnkell laughed madly. "There is no such thing as 'can't' here. They are dead. They killed one another, as viciously as rabid dogs. And now those strong enough to win are out there waiting for us, hiding in the shadows. They have hunted us, picking us off, one by one. We must fight our way out through the road."

The water around where Finn was standing began to ripple. Aein felt her mouth go dry. Finn saw it, too.

"Finn..." said Aein, holding out her hand to him. "Come to me."

Lars began to whine.

"This is what always happens," said Lord Arnkell as he backed up.

The surface of the water began to boil with air bubbles.

"FINN!" Aein cried.

He leapt as the jaws of a gigantic eel snapped right where he had been standing. The creature was the size of a cart. Finn hacked at it as it chased him to the bank of the clearing. The eel threw itself out of the water and onto the land, swiping Finn with its head and knocking him down. Finn's sword clattered out of his hand. Without a pause, Lars charged the eel and landed on its head, biting its eyes. The eel slithered backwards, flailing as it tried to throw Lars off, but the wolf had dug his teeth in deep. There was a crackling and popping sound. Fingers of lightning spread from the eel across the water. The heat singed the air. Lars's body convulsed and the eel tossed him aside before sliding away into the liquid depths of the swamp.

Heart in her throat, Aein ran to Lars's side. "He's breathing," she announced with relief as she stroked his head.

Finn rolled to his knees and grabbed his fallen sword. He used it to push himself up from the ground.

"This is what I am trying to tell you!" yelled Lord Arnkell, waving his hands impotently at where the sea monster disappeared.

"You win," said Finn, wincing as he limped over to Lars. "We'll stay away from the water."

Lars's eyes began to flutter open. "Thank the gods," said Aein, burying her face in his neck. His fur was crisp and smelled burned.

Finn reached down and rested his hand on the wolf's shoulder. "Too tough to die, that's what you are, Lars. When the balladeers sing your praises, it will be a song about that time you wrestled lightning and not even the gods could steal your thunder."

Lars rolled himself to standing with the panic of a downed animal. Though he was shaky, he kept his feet. He seemed completely uninterested in the praise of his brave deeds. He kept circling the clearing until the stunned look left his eyes.

The battle outside the clearing suddenly stopped. Lord Arnkell paled, rubbing his arm. "It is done. That creature has killed the last of my men."

There was a clacking sound on the road outside the clearing, and the boards groaned as if under a great weight. They all stood silent, not even daring to breathe, until it passed them and the noise faded to nothing.

"It's gone," whispered Lord Arnkell. "We need to leave before it comes back. We need to leave now."

Aein and Finn locked eyes and came to a silent decision. Queen Gisla commanded that if all was lost, to choose to hold the border. But it was time to acknowledge that this situation was well beyond the means of their army of three. Their deaths would be meaningless. The border was lost. Aein turned to Lars. "Can you lead us out?" she asked.

Though Lars eyed Lord Arnkell like he would rather make him lunch than help him, the wolf walked out of the clearing, sniffing the air for anything that might be in the shadows. Though Aein had her small knife, she realized she was going to need more. There was a stained and dirty sword next to one of the abandoned bedrolls. She picked it up. She might not be able to wield it well, but at least it was something. Finn found a discarded chainmail shirt and pulled it over his clothes. Lord Arnkell ran to one of the lanterns and held it to his chest, as if terrified to stand anywhere but in the protection of its light.

Lars gave a soft bark and Aein interpreted it as a sign the coast was clear. The remaining three walked out onto the wooden road. Immediately, they were shrouded in mist. There was a faint glow from the lantern, but she could not even see the shadows of the others. Aein brought her fingers up in front of her face. She saw nothing but fog.

"Grab onto one another," she instructed. Aein reached down and rested her hand on Lars's back, then Finn's hand rested on hers. "Everyone together?"

"I'm here," said Finn.

"And I," added the shaky voice of Lord Arnkell.

They walked on without a word. The fog pressed down and played the last sounds of the battle with the girtablilu. She heard Lord Arnkell stifle a terrified sob. She hoped his guards' screams of terror haunted his dreams.

Suddenly, she felt Finn trip and his hand left her. "Finn? Are you all right?" she asked. She searched the fog for him, but the moon's light could not pierce the gray.

"I'm here," he said.

She breathed deep. He grunted and placed his hand

back where it had been. She told her heart to stop beating like it was about to pound out of her chest. But then she realized it was not Finn behind her. The angle of the hand was wrong. It was too big. It came from a shoulder too tall. The fingertips had claws which tested her shoulder to figure out how thick her protection was. And the answer was she was not protected at all.

Without a word of warning, Aein took her blade and swung it against the arm. There came an inhuman scream. The arm fell to the ground. It was smooth like it was made from amphibian skin and it bled a tar-like substance.

"What was that?" she heard Finn cry from off in the distance.

"You are not following me!" warned Aein, striking out again and hitting something that sounded hollow like resin or wood. She could not see what it was. It was a glancing blow, nothing that could do any damage. It had been too long since she held a heavy sword and the sharp edge of the blade was wrong in her hand.

The furry body of Lars rushed past her thigh, his dog-like battle cry in his throat, snarling as he attacked whatever was in the mist. There was the ring of metal striking something hard and roars coming from the direction of Finn's voice. The mist parted just enough to show what was behind her.

It was the girtablilu.

It had been a trap.

The creature had pretended to go away to lure them out of the clearing.

His pointed, scorpion-like feet clattered on the wooden planks like hail. He was the color of midnight, his skin was slick and oily. Where she had cut off his arm, another was already growing in its place. Aein dodged to one side as his scorpion tail pierced the mist to strike her, hitting the ground directly where she had stood, then raised up to strike again. Lars leapt at the girtablilu and hung on. The creature's pincer-like front legs were snapping at Aein, but paused as the human half of the girtablilu took Lars by the scruff of his neck and threw him into the swamp. Lars struck a tree with a sickening crunch. Aein prayed that the water would not begin to ripple and boil.

The girtablilu advanced on Aein, claws clacking as he swiped at her, trying to cut her in two. She held the sword in two hands wondering how on earth she could kill this thing. She struck him again and again, but his armor was tougher than any steel. The only point of weakness was his upper torso and he would not let her near enough to strike him again.

Lars appeared out of nowhere and landed upon the girtablilu's back. The girtablilu began dancing in circles, trying to reach behind himself to grab the werewolf. The creature's venomous stinger struck Lars, burying itself deep in his pelt, again and again. Lars bled, but he did not let go, tearing at the creature's backbone with his powerful jaws.

And then the girtablilu struck out once more and missed, and when he missed, he struck himself instead. His stinger pierced his own back with such force, the tip went clean through and emerged in the front. The creature's face was puzzled as he looked down. His legs collapsed beneath him and he fell to one side, twitching.

And that was when Aein saw this monster had another weakness. On his underside where all the plates of his insect-like skeleton met, there was a soft spot, a spot which she might be able to pierce.

Lars was panting and wobbly. Even though he was immortal in wolf form, he needed time to recover, for his body to expel the venom injected into him.

A high-pitched scream pierced the air, coming from the direction of Finn and Lord Arnkell. She ran into the darkness towards the sound, hoping it was not the fog leading her in the wrong direction. Ahead, she saw the dim light from the lamp that Lord Arnkell had been carrying.

They were fighting another girtablilu, but this one's torso was shaped like a woman. Both Finn and Lord Arnkell were weary, unable to get inside its defenses. Aein dropped her sword and pulled the silver knife from her waistband.

"RUN!" Aein shouted as she came towards them.

Lord Arnkell picked up the lantern and headed one way. Finn ran the other. But Aein ran full tilt towards the girtablilu. The creature was distracted, not sure which one to follow. Aein fell onto her side and let the momentum carry her as she slid beneath it. The creature lifted its legs, sensing something wasn't right. But it was too late. With all her strength, Aein jammed the silver knife into the weak spot and prayed it worked.

The girtablilu let out a screeching cry and fell to its side, its legs scrabbling to reach the blade like a dying spider. Suddenly, Finn was there, grabbing Aein beneath her armpits and hauling her away from the sharp feet to safety. They stood, breath heaving as they watched the creature die. Aein was aware of Lars limping towards her and leaning against her body. She rested her hand on his fur until the girtablilu gasped and exhaled its last breath.

Silence fell over them as the fog began to thin.

She reached out to Finn. "Are you okay?" she asked.

He nodded, wiping his brow with the back of his hand. "I'll live."

Aein suddenly looked around, realizing they had lost one member of their party. "Where is Lord Arnkell?"

It was at that moment an eerie light filled the fog. It flickered golden and the wet mist was replaced with the smell of smoke and the sound of crackling wood.

Aein locked eyes with Finn in terror. They raced towards the flames.

They reached the edge of the swamp and ground to a halt. Lord Arnkell had dashed the lamp upon the boards, and the oil caught the ancient wood like paper. Lord

Arnkell had set the road on fire, trapping them inside. It was what they had all been trained to do if the border was ever breached. The bog surrounding the swamp would not allow any creature to pass. They had witnessed its grip the moment that time the horse had fallen off the road.

Lord Arnkell stood at the far end of the burn, his figure wavering in the heat.

The darkness of the night was beginning to lift as the sun began to rise.

"I'll tell everyone to burn their roads to contain the creatures of the swamp! I'll tell that queen of yours that you perished to save my life!" shouted Lord Arnkell. "The balladeers will sing songs of you three and how you led to my return! You are responsible for the glorious revolution I shall bring!" he shouted, holding his sword up high. "May your death be quick and painless!"

Aein, Finn, and Lars watched him as he walked away. They stood there watching him until the fire forced them back and they had to retreat into the swamp.

They ran in front of the flame, the road falling behind them into the water, leaping over the bodies of the creatures they had slain to save that traitorous man.

They reached the sacred clearing just as the sun rose and watched as the fire consumed the road just beyond the entrance. The soot and smoke brought tears of pain to Aein's eyes.

But the swamp did not burn. Only the road which would let them out.

Lars shifted back to himself, whole and healthy once again. He stood, facing Finn and Aein. He was terrified. He knew what it meant to be trapped in the swamp. He knew what madness would meet them here. He knew that within weeks, they would all be begging for death.

"What do we do?" he asked, unable to keep his voice steady.

Finn tried to infuse them with strength before the sun rose and stole his human form. "We travel to the Haidra

Kingdom through the swamp and we warn Queen Gisla that now Lord Arnkell has abandoned the border. Her war with him is now the least of her worries." But his words, for the first time, rang hollow.

Aein stared out into the swamp's forest, a land filled not just with the dangers that came across the border, but the wild werewolves who had rebelled against Lord Arnkell. Just beyond the clearing, the fog waited for them.

But it was at that moment, a hawk landed in a tree. He cocked his head and fixed his eyes upon Aein. There was intelligence there. The vision of Cook Bolstad filled her mind and his request, something so important he reached through the veil of death to ask her: to seek him out. Had he known secrets about the swamp no one else was aware of? Did he know these birds that watched them? Was there something else besides monsters here?

"The border is not abandoned," she said. "It must always be held by two, and by my count, we have three." She reached out to both Lars and Finn, grasping each of their hands in hers. "We travel to the Haidra Kingdom and we hold the border, just as the guard has always done. We survive."

The hawk flew a few branches away, as if beckoning her to follow.

"Besides," Aein added watching the creature. "I do not believe we are entirely alone."

ABOUT THE AUTHOR

Kate Danley is a *USA TODAY* Bestselling author and twenty-five year veteran of stage and screen with a B.S. in theatre from Towson University. She was one of four students to be named a Maryland Distinguished Scholar in the Arts.

Her debut novel, *The Woodcutter* (published by 47North), was honored with the Garcia Award for the Best Fiction Book of the Year, 1st Place Fantasy Book in the Reader Views Literary Awards, and the winner of the Sci-Fi/Fantasy category in the Next Generation Indie Book Awards. Her book *Maggie for Hire* hit the *USA Today* Bestselling list as part of the boxed set *Magic After Dark* and has been optioned for film and television development. *Queen Mab* was honored with the McDougall Previews Award for Best Fantasy Book of the Year and was named the 1st Place Fantasy Book in the Reader Views Reviewers Choice Awards.

Her plays have been produced in New York, Los Angeles, Seattle, and Maryland. Her screenplay *Fairy Blood* won 1st Place in the Breckenridge Festival of Film Screenwriting Competition in the Action/Adventure Category.

Her scripts *The Playhouse, Dog Days, Sock Zombie, SuperPout*, and *Sports Scents* can be seen in festivals and on the internet. She trained in on-camera puppetry with Mr. Snuffleupagus and recently played the head of a 20-foot dinosaur on an NBC pilot. She has over 300+ film, theatre, and television credits to her name.

She lost on Hollywood Squares.

Coming Fall 2015

Sign up for the Kate Danley newsletter to be the first to hear about the finale to the *Twilight Shifters* series

http://www.katedanley.com/subscribe.html

Other Kate Danley Books

The Woodcutter
Queen Mab

Maggie MacKay: Magical Tracker
Maggie for Hire
Maggie Get Your Gun
Maggie on the Bounty
M&K Tracking
The M-Team

O'Hare House Mysteries
A Spirited Manor
Spirit of Denial
Distilled Spirits
In High Spirits

Twilight Shifters
The Dark of Twilight
Moon Rise
Light of Dawn

www.katedanley.com

Printed in Great Britain
by Amazon